Alannah

For Shayla—
may magic always
be a part of your life!

Leslie Brooks

Alannah

LESLIE BROOKS

Alannah

For information about permission to reproduce selections from this book,
write to: Permissions, Love Incarnate Books,
Post Office Box 111, Colrain, Massachusetts 01340

Book design by Robin Brooks
Typeface, Adobe Jenson Pro
Cover Painting by Ruth Sanderson
Production management by Love Incarnate Books

ISBN 978-0-996-6523-2-2
Library of Congress Control Number: 2016905376
Love Incarnate Books, Colrain, MA

Published by Love Incarnate Books
www.love-incarnate.com

To children everywhere,
and the child inside each of us,
who will always believe in magic.

Other Books by the Author

Love Incarnate Series (Spirituality)

Love Incarnate:
I have come to tell a story of love

On the Path of the Beloved

Soul Writer

Table of Contents

Acknowledgments

I thank all readers young and old—as well as my own soul—who together bring magic to my life. When we believe in magic, we believe in ourselves. Life is about magic and doing what we love to do best!

I also thank Ann McNelly for the loving ease and grace she brings to editing, and also for some of her delightful comments! Not every editor writes in the margins, "I want a dragon!"

So much gratitude too, to Ellen Eller who edited the final touches and polished it into the book that it is!

I thank also my dear friend Sylvia Orcutt who took the time to read my manuscript and to be honest with me.

Thanks also to my twin sister Robin Brooks for all of her loving patience in helping me with the design.

And I am always grateful to my dear teacher, mentor, soul sister, friend, and fellow "white witch" Moriah Marston, to whom I read out loud the chapters as they first came into being. I know that from the place where she is now with the masters, she is thrilled to see this in physicality at last!

—Leslie Brooks

1 *The Story Begins*

The old one rocks herself by the hearth gently, so as not to wake the child in her lap. A circle of children sits at her feet, fidgeting and restless because the story has not yet begun, but knowing that, from this old one, it will be *true*. There is a faraway look in her eyes as she draws the tale from her memory, and then, her face wreathed in a smile, she looks into the eyes of each child, one by one, and begins to weave the story into their souls.

"In a place called *Far Away*, and a time called *Long Ago*, there once lived a woodcutter and his wife, in a simple hut like this one, in a hamlet in the woods. They were happy but for the fact that they had no child. Nearby, around a plain and halfway up a mountain, towered a mighty castle where lived the king and queen of the land. They too longed for a child.

"And long before that *Long Ago*, and far beyond that *Far Away*, in a place of deepest magic hovering beyond the mists and veils of time itself, there was talk of change. And so the story begins."

Alannah

The child on her lap wakes and looks up into her eyes. The children sitting on the sweet smelling, herb-strewn floor draw closer, their eyes widening to hear more. And the old one continues the tale.

In that place of deepest magic, a great gathering occurred, of ascended masters, minor gods and god-
desses, witches and wizards, faeries and dragons.
One who took part was a white witch—a sorceress. And one
who listened was the soul of a child.

All those in attendance were filled with love, light, and
magic, as well as some little mischief. It was they who spoke
of change. They foresaw what was to come and infused the
path of the child's destiny with all the powers they could
muster. And yet they knew that the Source of all things
would in the end prevail, placing love and joy before all else,
while still allowing for learning to occur.

Merlin, the greatest of wizards, was one in the circle
gathered there. He decreed, *The child shall be spun of joy and
goodness, light and laughter and love, but the foremost of these
will be joy.*

The reigning queen of the faeries came forward and
added, *And I bequeath to her the blood of the most ancient magic
of all times, that of the faery and dragon realms.*

In this place of ethers and veils, the naming occurred also—an invocation of the power and magic of the child who would come. It was decreed by those in the circle, in the light language of magic, *She is to be named Alannah. It is a naming of not just a child but a new era for the planet, for its meaning is "that which is precious." It is made up of the sacred "ah" sound of the heart, for love and compassion.*

Across the land, long before she was born, the sound of her name began to be breathed and whispered and entrained into the very beings of the planet, silently, invisibly, and unconsciously across the universes, preparing for her coming.

It was decreed also by those who gathered that she must learn her magic in secret, hidden from those in power—the king, the queen, the court. Yet, when the time was right, she must be of the royal blood of the kingdom to manifest the change to its completion.

As the dawn of her birth drew nigh, the ingredients of her creation gathered from out of the ethers and spun and wove themselves into the very being of who she would become and, again, the foremost of these was joy.

Many months before the night of the birthing, a wise woman visited the woodcutter Jacob and his wife Anna. She told them that the goodwife would at last bear a child, a son, who would be raised as the prince of the land.

She added that, that same night, the boy-child would be removed and replaced by a girl-child who would be the true princess, but whom they would raise as their own. She would be such a child as they had never known, a child of magic and wonder and delight. And all was to be kept secret, for the sake of the land, the planet, and the people.

The couple looked at each other, knowing that the wise woman spoke *true,* and they accepted what was. They had prayed and hoped for many years and would be glad of any child to raise as their own. The wise woman told them little more but that the babe must be nurtured and loved and kept safe. The man and his wife nodded their heads, unable to speak for their joy.

3 Secret in the Woods

One night, the darkest night of the year, there was secret movement in the forest, scampering, leaping, crawling and flying to a place where all gathered in the trees by the hut of the woodcutter and his wife.

Along the plain and up the mountain, other creatures gathered in and around the castle. Mice crept from their gnawed holes to hide beneath the royal bed. Mourning doves, owls, bats, and starlings crowded the stone ledges outside the royal sleeping chamber. Snakes and voles and woodchucks were drawn from their safe underground holes in the orchards and gardens, and crept to the castle walls.

The air trembled. There was a tingling—a feeling of expectancy—in the hearts of the creatures and, around them, a growing magic of tides and winds and shooting stars that spread throughout the universe. A hush descended upon the land and, in the dark gloaming time just before dawn, the hour of the deepest magic, all waited breathless.

If you had been listening with your soul's ears, as the world slept that night, you might have heard the excited murmurings and whisperings in the stars and winds, in the trees and caves and tunnels. If you had been watching with your soul's eyes, you might have seen the tiptoed gathering of magical creatures, standing or sitting on their haunches in the moonlit, snow-bound winter land of woods, and in the castle gardens and royal sleeping chamber.

In the waiting, in the darkness, a comet soared across the sky, breathing the magical child into being. The faintest light spread across the mountain and grew in palest corals until, finally, through the bare trees, the sun tipped its brilliant face above the horizon.

And so it was that the long-awaited child was born to the king and queen of the land—a beautiful little girl. Her joyous cry rang like a clear bell across the mountains, heralding a new day and a new era for the land.

Unicorns and dragons, ascended masters and faery queens all danced in attendance, invisible yet real regardless, for this one moment. Then all returned to a semblance of normalcy, though nothing would ever be normal again.

At the same moment, another child, a boy-child—not of magic, but destined still—was born to the woodcutter's wife. And then immediately after the births, time stopped.

A sparkling stream of magic descended from the stars and swirled and spiraled and wrapped itself around the two babes and lifted them up into the ethers and set them down, one by one, the girl-child to the hut now, and the boy-child to the castle—all silently, all invisibly.

Those in attendance—the ladies in waiting to the queen, and the hamlet women with the woodcutter's wife— shook their heads, as if trying to clear them, and then simply shrugged, no longer trusting their eyes.

Only the castle midwife saw the tiny butterfly mark, the mark that proved a birthright, behind the tiny perfectly formed ear of the true princess. But no one would learn her secret for, that same morning, she was whisked away by magic to a land far away to live out the rest of her life.

There was one other, a white witch—a sorceress—who saw all in a crystal globe in her castle tower. And she rejoiced that the time had come at last, as it was written long ago.

Thus it happened that, in a hamlet in the woods lying near the base of a mountain, so close to the castle that no one would guess she might be hidden there, the newborn princess slept in a sheepskin by a lowly hearth. And the woodcutter's son slept in cloth of gold and silk in the castle.

$\mathcal{4}$ *T r u e*

The morning after her birth, while all the hamlet lay sleeping, the tiny infant girl awoke and looked around with her newborn eyes, seeing and not seeing, human and not human. Her rough-hewn cradle, made lovingly by the woodcutter, rested beneath the one window of the hut, a skin covering it to keep out the cold.

She watched as tiny faery hands pulled back a corner of the skin to reveal a wonder of stars against the great black night. Faeries fluttered in and surrounded her, giggling, and clumsily and excitedly spilled their dust and themselves wherever they landed, knowing who she was, and eager for what was to come.

Joy surged through her little chest and all through her body, making her coo in delight at the beauty she beheld that felt so familiar, like the place she came from. And with each surging of joy, she heard a faint sound of tinkling bells floating all around her, whispering the word *true.*

As a tiny baby, yet without human language, she did not know this as a word. She imagined it was a sound the faeries made. But as she grew older and learned to speak, she realized that the faeries made lots of sounds—giggles and laughter and chattering. It was only at certain times, like when she felt joy, that she heard this word *true* whispered. She did not know where it came from or why, but it was so.

As she grew, she began to hear more, like the wind whispering, *Is it true? Listen to your whole being.* When there was a rightness in what she was doing or saying or thinking, she found that this rightness felt like that same tingling all through her, and she knew it was *true*. She didn't know yet what *true* meant, fully, but she knew it was about more than just right or wrong.

And when the joy surged in her, with the feeling of *true* that came with it, there was something else too, like a memory from long ago that she couldn't quite grasp, that had in it a feeling of urgency, something she must do.

5 The Ride

Five summers passed. One night, Alannah was sleeping on her pallet by the hearth. Her dream self woke and lifted out of her solid little body. She floated out the door on a song without sound that filled the air all around her. It was a song she knew but couldn't remember. Somehow, she knew it was a part of her, just as she knew she must follow wherever it went.

Silently, she drifted like a wraith through the sleeping village into the woods nearby. The moon was full, and the stars were out, and the world was asleep. Magic wound and wrapped around her legs, like a purring cat. Only the whisper of her steps and the whoosh of her skirt told her she was real.

No humans, but other creatures watched, as tiny flowers, greyed by moonlight, grew in her every footfall. She moved up the forest path, not knowing this was so. Her sweet baby face was smudged with ashes from the fire, or was it faery dust? Only the faeries knew for sure.

Her pale gold ringlets bouncing with every step, her grey eyes opened wide in wonder and excitement, for she knew where the song was leading her, but she did not know why. It was taking her to the wildflower meadow at the top of the path, where in light of day she ran and played and picked flowers in the breezes with the faeries all around her.

It is not daytime now, she thought. *Who has called me? Who has asked me to come?*

She was an obedient little girl because that was her way, and so she went where she was called. She was also a very loving child. Often, she'd pat the cheeks of her mother or father with her chubby little hands, as she climbed onto their laps. Or she'd stand looking up into their eyes lovingly, hands resting on the knees of one or the other, as they sat before the hearth.

Tonight though, it was not her parents who called. *Who is it?* she wondered again, not afraid, simply asking.

Coming to the end of the path, she hummed the song to herself, and inexplicably, it stirred a feeling of joy in her heart, a feeling she knew, like *true*. She passed between the last few great ones. The great ones were the big forest trees that had been there for centuries and had talked to her of their silence and wisdom and all that they knew. She entered the meadow that was circled by even more great ones, rising up to the very stars.

And she gasped. She stopped breathing for a moment. Her little heart pattered.

For there, on the far side of the clearing, looking up at the night sky too, not knowing she was there yet—or pretending not to know—its great tail trailing the ground, was a mighty blue-black dragon, so dark it almost disappeared into the dark of the night trees and the dark of the night sky, almost but not quite.

Alannah heard a whispered *true,* and she knew she was safe, but still she clenched her little fists in her skirts.

"*Oh!*" she whispered. "*Oh!*" She knew she mustn't jump up and down, not even a tiny bit. The dragon must be very proud, it was so big, and what would it want with a little girl anyway? "*But, oh!*" she whispered again. "*Oh! If only . . .*"

The dragon twisted its long neck a quarter turn and bent its head down to look at her. It was as if the song without sound reached right into the little girl's heart and filled it with a spreading golden warmth, and that gave her courage.

She looked up into the eyes of the dragon. They were like silver stars, they were so far away, yet she felt herself drawn right into them. She moved her tiny feet, one by one, and tiptoed slowly across the meadow until she stood just below the great head of the beast, her little heart beating faster than ever now.

She had to bend all the way backwards and crane her head all the way up to even see the dragon's head right above her, he was so tall. And then she did what long afterwards she thought might have been a very silly thing. She reached her chubby little hand, as high as she could, up to the dragon's big scaly foreleg at the bottom of his shin, and she patted him.

Suddenly, the great head swung down in a mighty arc, almost to the ground. He looked right into her eyes. Without hesitating, Alannah smiled and looked into his.

Now, this dragon and this little girl had known each other for lifetimes, but not this lifetime yet. She was brand new, and he was very old. Even though he had known her before, he was shocked to his very core to see her complete trust in him so soon. Even though it was his song that called her here—the song they'd shared over lifetimes—he hadn't expected this.

"Oh!" she cried out loud, this time seeing the love and wonder in his eyes. "Oh! I thought you called me so I could ride! Couldn't I please have a ride? Please? I would so love to be friends! I would so love to fly! Couldn't we, please?"

Without words, without sound, she saw his answer, for his long neck bent even farther down so that it lay right along the ground now. He waited patiently while she scrambled up and wrapped her little arms flat along it, as she again cried, "Oh!" She tried very hard not to bounce up and down in her excitement.

For the first time, the dragon did make a sound then, that she could hear with her physical ears. It was a low groan that rumbled and vibrated through her whole being. Somehow, she knew with a knowing that she didn't question, that he had been trying very hard to hold most of his sound in, for if it had been any louder, it would have shattered the earth. Now she saw why he didn't make sound before.

She giggled. She was completely delighted. So was he, for he had loved and protected her for centuries through many wars and peacetimes, as she had done for him also, although she did not know or remember that.

Slowly, he rose on his hind legs, lifting himself to his full height and again, she cried, "Oh!" even louder this time, for she was in the treetops now, and they were still on the ground! Just as she thought this, he trundled to the center of the clearing, slowly spread his great wings filling the span of the meadow, and then he lifted off the ground, circled the meadow, and rose above the trees.

Up, up, up, they went, soaring above the hamlet, above the castle grounds, and then into the very stars themselves. The little girl held tight, her breath swept away by the speed of the flight, and her eyes round as the moon.

Even though the span of her little arms in no way reached around the dragon's neck, his magic kept her from falling, and he was especially careful this first flight that this was so. The little girl did not know that the magic of her love for him also helped to keep her safe.

They flew over mountains and rivers. They swooped up and swerved down and circled and spiraled and flipped over and over. All that time, Alannah held on, sometimes speechless, sometimes whooping for joy. She could feel her little chest hugging the dragon's powerful neck, and she knew that this was a place where she belonged.

All the while they were flying, the dragon was whispering to her without words, through the song without sound, telling her of her magic and who she was for *true.* She listened, taking it all in silently, making pictures of what he said in the invisible places inside of her, knowing that some day she would understand. She smiled secretly to herself, and her heart was glad and also a little afraid.

Sometimes, they flew so close to the trees that streams of faeries flitted around and by them, racing them as if to a finish line. They passed right through a rainbow on the other side of the planet where the sun was now up, and through a rainstorm, and then a desert to dry. The dragon showed her other countries, other peoples, other ways of living. She was glad to see them, for each new and different thing she saw, she stored inside, to keep for later, not knowing why.

At last, she yawned, and the dragon knew it was time to go home. He slowed his flight, descended from the stars, spiraled down one last time, and gently landed where they had begun. The moon had set, and there was the faintest blush on the eastern horizon as the little girl stumbled sleepily off the dragon's neck and kissed him goodbye.

The next thing she knew she was waking by the hearth of the hut where she lived. She gasped, wondering if it was all a dream, but then she looked down at the palms of her hands and knew that the faint silvery dust on them came from her dragon's scales, which she had clung to all night, and she knew that it was *true*.

She smiled to herself, added a small fistful of peat to the fire and slipped back into her little bed, gently drifting to sleep, murmuring her dragon's name—Dante.

Over the months and years that followed, Alannah went to Dragon Meadow and continued to ride Dante. Each time, he told her more of her magic and slowly, over time, even untrained, her magic grew.

6 *T h e   P r i n c e*

Up in the castle on top of the mountain, the wood-cutter's boy—now prince—passed five summers also, and how different they were from those of the child Alannah.

Named Tarek for "morning star," the prince grew sturdy and robust with bright rosy cheeks and sparkling, laughing eyes. He astonished the courtiers and king's advisors with his natural immunity to all their efforts to win him to their sides. As young as he was, they vied for his friendship, hoping for any future power and riches he might bestow.

Despite the fact that, early on, as a babe in lacy dresses, he was fed with golden cups and silver spoons, and cared for by an army of nannies, nurses and under-nurses, he remained somehow innocent and unspoiled.

First crawling, later toddling and running, he was drawn to the birds and frogs, rabbits and foxes that managed to wander into the immaculately manicured knot gardens and sculpted hedges of the castle grounds.

In short pants, he rolled his hoop, laughing, along the garden paths and fell over himself to pick up a fallen flower, or to follow with his eyes the fickle path of a butterfly, or the laborious one of a ladybug. He was fascinated with every creature and every nuance of the natural world around him.

As he grew, he learned to love his kingdom. He learned to love the people and, somehow, they recognized that love, and they loved him back, though he did not know it. He only saw how they looked at the king and queen when he was allowed to ride with them in the royal carriage, followed by the royal entourage.

He saw how the people, though doffing their caps and curtseying, did not look up as the royal family passed, but seemed rather to keep their heads down. He wanted to know what they hid. As young as he was, he told himself, *I will come back here and see. I want to know these people.* There was a feeling inside him, in his belly, that he didn't understand. It made him feel a little sick because he felt there was something he must do, but he didn't know what.

As a youngster in the carriage, he would ask the king and queen, "Why don't they smile? Why don't they look at us?" and "What are they doing?" and "Where are we?" Finally, the queen—loving him so, as their only child—would say gently, "That's enough now. No more questions," without giving him any answers at all.

He would fall silent then, at least for a little while, his entire little body bristling in readiness for the end of what might be the acceptable amount of time passed for him to ask more.

There was so much he wanted to know. There was so much he cared about. No one in the court could understand how it had come about that to this king and this queen could be born a prince who defied, through his very nature, the seemingly complacent generations that came before him.

The king and queen were kind and good people, and it seemed that their advisors took advantage of that goodness. The council of advisors did their best to line their own pockets and their own stores of provisions, robbing the land and the people of what was rightfully theirs. For some reason, the king and queen seemed to have no power over them.

Little Tarek didn't understand any of this at first. He just knew—seemed to sense—that something was wrong. As soon as the carriage returned to the castle, he would run to the castle stables and call for the stable master. Rannulf was a gruff, shaggy old soldier who sometimes picked Tarek up by the scruff of his neck and shook him to slow him down.

"We must go now, Rannulf!" the prince would cry. "You must saddle my pony now, while the people are still out there!"

"Just hold your ponies, young Tarek," Rannulf would say calmly. "We are not going anywhere until you tell me where we are going, and what you are planning, and what made you want to go in the first place."

"I must go back and see the people we just passed on the road. There is something wrong. I know it! I want to talk with them. Please, hurry. We must go!"

Rannulf knew what the prince had seen. He knew the lay of the land. It was not for him to say, but he also knew that in this boy—this prince—there was hope for the kingdom. He knew that he, a mere stable master, could help the kingdom he loved by taking the prince where he wanted to go, while maintaining his silence.

So he would agree to take Tarek on these wild rides to the villages and hamlets and the far-off forests. First, though, he would insist that the prince calm down, think for a moment, and then speak slowly and clearly of what he wanted—for two reasons. The first was that, in the telling, came a certain warmth to Rannulf's heart and hope in his mind that the people would have a champion at last.

The second reason was that, in his own wise way and looking at this boy as nearest to a son as could be, Rannulf knew he was helping to shape the king that the prince would one day become.

Rannulf insisted that Tarek wear the clothes of a stable boy and that they go out of the castle grounds by different means every time, hidden and cloaked. Rannulf knew that, otherwise, they would be stopped by the spies of the king's advisors with poison-honey questions and cold-eyed smiles, and they would have to turn back, and the prince would have learned nothing.

And so it came about that, among the people of the land, word was whispered from ear to ear, and hamlet to hamlet—throughout all the far-off places in the mountains and forests, to the very boundaries of the kingdom—that from time to time there might appear a young boy dressed in simple peasant clothes, riding a pony, accompanied by a gruff, surly, grey-bearded man.

No one was to say out loud that they knew that this boy was the prince. They kept the secret, and they loved him for it. They loved him for coming to them and asking gently and shyly what their lives were like.

He would politely walk up to a cottage and knock on the door and wait for the door to open. When it did, he would ask if he might come in for a visit. And of course, the cottage dwellers were astonished at the friendliness of this boy who they knew was the prince, although they never once let on.

They would offer him a mug of small beer and a crust of bread and ask him to sit down. He would shyly accept, knowing it would be impolite not to do so, and then he would ask to see their gardens and any handiwork about the place.

As prince, he was kept so separate from things of the everyday life of the people that he was fascinated by whatever they might show him. Sometimes, he'd play with the children of the family, getting muddy and tearing his clothes, just like any boy his age, and this too endeared him to the people.

There was a wisdom about him beyond his years, and word of this wisdom spread across the kingdom. It gave hope to the people at last.

7 *The Trolls*

From time to time, Alannah saw the prince from afar, in the royal carriage with his parents the king and queen, but she gave little thought to him. Sometimes, something nagged her memory about the prince, something deep inside from long ago. Mostly, though, she gave no thought to the prince or the mountain beyond the plain where the castle lay—the world outside her little world of hamlet woods and dragon meadow.

Four years passed, and Alannah was nine years old now.

With the help of Dante, her dragon, she stumbled into her magic and played with it, harmlessly making flowers appear and disappear, turning faery dust into daisy chains, and thinking small animals to her side. Sometimes, she swept the hearth without lifting a finger, but her magic was small and delightful and fun, for now anyway.

Early on, she thought everyone had magic and believed in it. She discovered the truth later.

This day, she was skipping across the meadow, singing to herself, "I have magic! I love magic! Magic is for me!" and giggling, just for fun. She spotted an iridescent blue butterfly flitting from flower to flower and stalk to stalk, until it disappeared into the forest, and so she ran after it, following it deep into the woods, humming to herself.

Whenever she hummed, it was the same tune, the song without sound that Dante sang, and it filled her heart with joy.

Suddenly, she heard a hissing "sh-sh-sh-sh!" She stopped in her tracks and looked around but saw no one. She walked to the nearest bush and lifted its boughs and looked underneath, but there was no one there. She peeked behind the near trees. Still no one. Finally, walking more slowly now, not skipping any more, she again followed the path, and the butterfly seemed to be following it too.

Soon, Alannah saw the path had a fork she'd never seen before. She stopped. She looked at it. *I wonder where it goes,* she thought to herself. She pressed her little index finger into her cheek and thought for a moment. She loved to explore, and maybe she'd find some new friends. So far, everyone she had ever met was friendly to her and kind.

Tentatively at first, and then with growing curiosity and excitement, she followed the new path. There were the same kinds of trees and bushes, the same sounding birdcalls and patter of animals. But as the path wound downhill, it got quieter. And the trees seemed closer together.

Deeper and deeper into the woods they went, until the blue butterfly stopped on a tree trunk, its wings fanning up and down, up and down, slowly, as if waiting for her. Absent-mindedly, she hummed her little tune under her breath, watching the butterfly. Then she began to breathe the words slowly, singing them softly, "I can make magic. I can do magic. I can make—"

Again, she heard the hissing "sh-sh-sh-sh," and she stopped singing and looked around her, startled.

The tree trunk where the blue butterfly waited was very thick across, wider than she could reach with both arms out-stretched. It was old and gnarled and reached its limbs so high into the sky that, even leaning back as far as she could, Alannah couldn't see the top.

She sang tentatively, just to see, "I can make—" and, im-mediately, she heard the "sh-sh-sh-sh" again, and it seemed to come from the tree itself.

Just then the blue butterfly lifted off and flew around the trunk. Alannah followed tiptoeing, and her eyes grew wide as they lit upon an opening on the other side. The butterfly waited there, its wings fanning up and down, and then it flew inside. Alannah took a deep breath, stepped in after it, and found that the opening continued down, deep into the earth.

She carefully climbed down the rungs of roots, holding tight, as the path spiraled down, getting darker as it went but for the pale blue glow of the butterfly. She was not afraid. Down and down she went until finally she made the last bend and came to the floor. She was in a vast dark wet cave whose walls were made of earth bound in roots. There before her were the creatures who said "sh-sh-sh-sh."

Their heads were big and round, and what little hair they had was sparse and wispy. They had big pointed ears, big eyes, long skinny arms and legs, and short bodies with bellies that stuck out. Their skin was the color of clay. The only clothing they wore was made of fur wrapped around their middles.

There were eight of them, all sitting in the same way on their haunches, all rubbing their hands together. They each put a long skinny finger up in front of their mouths and said, as one, "Sh-sh-sh-sh."

"Why do you stop my song?" asked Alannah. "I AM magic! It's *true*! I CAN make—"

"Sh-sh-sh-sh," they said, again as one, although she noticed now there was a twinkle in their eyes, of mischief maybe, or devilishness.

Or is it evil? she wondered to herself. *But what is "evil"?* She had never heard that word before, but somehow she had a feeling of what it meant. *So, no, not evil,* she told herself firmly, for they were new friends. Maybe they were just what her mother had called "misguided."

Then a thought she had never had before came to her: *What if I fail in your magic?* she heard. She looked up, startled again. They were all smiling at her now, and nodding their heads at her and each other, wisely, as if they had put the thought there themselves.

"But I CAN do magic! I love magic!" Alannah persisted, trying to be brave.

"No, you can't," said one of the trolls, for that is what they were. "We don't want you to. So you can't, and you mustn't, and you aren't allowed to. We just plain don't want you to."

"And anyway," another added, "we don't believe you at all."

Alannah's whole life was about believing, in her magic, in her parents, in the goodness all around her, in everything that existed! And now here were these new friends—she had always believed that all beings were her friends—telling her that they didn't believe she could do magic.

This is most curious, she thought to herself but was too polite to say so. "Why don't you believe I can do magic?" she asked politely instead. "Why don't you?"

"Because," said yet another, and he looked to be the oldest of them all, "because we don't want you to. We don't want the world to hope that magic exists. We don't like hope. It's better without it."

"But why?"

They grumbled and mumbled amongst themselves, scratching their heads. Finally, the same elder said, "Because we have always thought this way, and we don't believe in change. We don't like it."

"But why?" asked Alannah. "There is so much goodness and love in the world, and so much that is *true.* I don't mean to be impolite, but how can you be happy thinking that way?"

In her being, Alannah began to grow an awareness of another world, a place that was not of the *true* that she knew. A feeling like sadness started to come over her, and her heart ached with it. She didn't know what to do, she felt so sad for these creatures. She wanted to help them, the way she always wanted to help people or animals—whoever came into her path.

Again, they grumbled and mumbled among themselves and scratched their heads, and this time they shifted uncomfortably. It seemed that the youngest of them was arguing rather strongly. It was he this time who interrupted the argument the loudest by saying, "But we're not happy! We've never been happy! And we have no idea what happy means!"

"Oh. I am so sorry," whispered Alannah. She thought for a minute, her heart almost breaking now, her sadness so deep and so strong she had to rock back and forth on her feet to comfort herself, as she tried to think of a way through for herself, and for them.

And then she came to a decision. Slowly, she walked up to the eldest of the trolls, and she placed her hand ever so gently on his arm. And she said, "I'm sorry again to seem impolite, but you see, when you talk like that, it makes me feel very sad. Is there anything I can do to help you? It would make me happy if there was something I could do for you."

The old wrinkled troll looked at her. He looked down at his big ugly feet. He looked at his ugly companions. He looked at her sweet kind face, and it dawned on him that she might mean what she said. Never before had someone said something like this to him. Always, he had been ugly.

Always, it had been the duty of his kind to exact tolls at bridges in the middle of nowhere and, wherever they had done this, they had encountered anger and resentment. Always, he and his kind had been shunned, and no one had ever spoken to them, other than to tell them to go away.

A strange feeling, a warmth, began to spread across his chest. He didn't know what it was, but something like an echo of a memory from long ago whispered inside him that he liked this feeling, and that it was—if he dared even think it—good.

Then something far stranger happened. As she strengthened her hold on his arm, gently, just a little, something began to cloud his vision. It was moisture in his eye. He looked at her, and she saw a tear forming there and said, very simply, and quietly, "Thank you," and she smiled a tremulous smile.

His voice breaking, he cried, shabbily, full of shame, "How can you be thanking me? I have done nothing! It is you who brought me this feeling in my chest! It is you who wet my eye! How can you have anything to thank me for?"

"I, well, I-I-I'm thanking you for letting me love you, I think," replied Alannah. None of the trolls knew how it could be that such a little girl could speak such words of wisdom.

"I-I, well, I love to love, you see. Will you be my friend? Will all of you be my friends? I would so love that."

The old troll burst out sobbing and hid his face in his hands. The other trolls wrapped themselves around him in a circle and mumbled and grumbled too, all crying now. They mumbled and grumbled because that was their way, but what they were really saying was that this was something new. They were not opposed to it. That, in itself, was something new too.

When at last they turned around and looked at Alannah, as a group, they were all smiling shyly, but mostly looking at their big ugly toes. Then all was quiet, for no one could think of anything to say. Alannah was embarrassed that she might have said too much, and they were shy because their feelings were new, and they didn't know what to do with them.

Finally, the youngest one said, "Do you really want to be our friend?" And he looked down at his feet again.

"Yes, I do," answered Alannah. "I would like to be friends, if you might want that too. Do you?"

They all mumbled and grumbled, and somehow the words they were saying sounded like "yes."

"But what does that mean?" asked the youngest one who seemed to be the least shy. "What do we do?"

"Well, um," thought Alannah out loud. "Maybe you could show me around your home and tell me what you like to eat?"

"Like?" asked the eldest. "We don't like anything! I mean, oh . . . . Well, I suppose we do like to eat worms, and fungus is very tasty. Perhaps, you'd like to try it?"

After seeing Alannah's face in response to this suggestion, despite her polite intentions, the trolls decided to show her their cave. It had many passages leading off the main cave, hewn of rock and dirt bound in roots, and rounded chambers.

One passage they passed without going into, and she asked, "Where does this one go?"

They mumbled and grumbled, and finally the youngest one, whose name was Dorin, again arguing with the others, seemed at last to win the argument. He turned to her, saying, "We will show you." They led her down the passage to a thick oak door blackened with age, with iron hinges, the only door in any of the passages that Alannah had seen so far. Dorin stepped aside to make way for the eldest troll. "Grandfather, will you open it please?" he asked.

The old one's look softened when he was called this name, and Alannah noticed this. He looked at her and said, "Yes, he is my grandson. Hard to believe he is so stubborn, isn't it?" There was a twinkle in his eye, when he said this, as if he wasn't stubborn himself! "My name is Selwik, but when he calls me so, there is nothing I wouldn't do for him, and he knows it!" Again, the twinkle.

Alannah smiled at him and wondered what it would be like to have a grandfather or a grandmother, and for the first time wondered why she didn't know them.

Selwik turned to the door, mumbled something—a few strange words—and an old black wrought iron key appeared in his hand. He put it in the lock and, after some squeaking and mumbling and grumbling of its own, the door slowly opened. He led the way into the chamber and the others followed, standing to one side. Alannah paused at the entrance, her eyes round with surprise.

"I thought you didn't believe in magic," she said. "I don't understand."

"I used to have magic," said Selwik, "and I still use it to open this door and for a few other things, but I don't want the world to know about magic, because it can be dangerous."

"But how?" asked Alannah.

"I have seen magic used for dangerous purposes. Why do you think we live here, down under the ground? We were banished here long ago, and it is our plight to remain."

"But don't you like it here?" asked Alannah. "Isn't this your home now?"

"Yes, but still . . . someday you will understand. That's all I will say about it," he ended firmly, and he beckoned her into the room.

She entered and looked around. This chamber was bigger than the others. On all sides, stacked high and falling over each other so there was barely room to stand, were barrels and coffers and caskets of all sizes, all old as time, with clasps of dulled bronze or copper or silver beneath the color of their aging.

"What is all this?" she cried.

"It is our takings, of course!" answered Selwik, with a grin that cracked across his face. He took another key out of nowhere and unlocked one of the caskets and threw the lid open. It was overflowing with gold pieces. Then he opened another and another—all the ones on top—and all were full of gold.

"What do you mean?" she asked, after a stunned silence.

"This is our garnering! It is the law of the land that we exact a toll at every bridge! Surely you know that! That has always been the duty of the trolls since time began!"

"But why is it all still here? Why haven't you spent it? There is so much! You could have warm clothes and . . . Oh, I'm sorry. I didn't mean to be rude. I'm sure you have your own reasons."

"We don't like to spend it. We already have everything we need. We like to count it," said Dorin quietly, shrugging.

"Oh," replied Alannah, and then she was very quiet herself and looked down at her feet.

"What are you thinking, girl?" asked Selwik.

"Well, if you don't want to spend it and, if you already have everything you need, couldn't you maybe give some of it away to people who could really use it?" Then, she gulped and, stepping closer to Selwik, she again placed her hand on his arm.

For a moment, there was complete silence in the chamber, as Selwik looked at her hand there. The group watched his expressions change from irritation to softening to puzzlement and then wonder. His eyes opened wide, staring at nothing, as he seemed to remember something, as if waking from a long sleep.

"The mark of the butterfly," he said, as if in a trance. And then he looked up at her, astonished. He quickly reached out his arm to push the others aside, climbed up and scrambled over one of the piles of caskets and coffers and began to move them aside, one by one, searching deliberately until he picked up something small.

"Ah, yes. Here it is," he said, straightening up.

He held a box of carved wood small enough to fit in the palm of his hand. Letters and symbols were inlaid in tarnished silver all over the surface of the box. "Hold out your hand, girl," he said gruffly and, as she did so, he placed the box there while mumbling some words, and the box opened by itself.

Inside, the tiniest of pearls filled the box and began to move out of the way so that the *true* jewel could show, a rare sapphire that only magic could have wrought into the shape of a butterfly. It was intricately etched with symbols from another world, another time. Alannah gasped.

"It's beautiful!" she cried.

"Yes, and you must guard it with your life," said Selwik.

"But why are you giving it to me? I am just a hamlet girl. What if I lose it?"

"You won't. It is yours now. Long ago, when I was a wee lad, my great-grandfather was still alive. He showed this to me and told me to keep it hidden until the time was right, and I would know when that was.

"I had forgotten about it until now, and I don't even know why I remember it, except that something about you reminded me. Somehow, the magic is telling me that the time is right, and you are the one to have it. Will you keep it safe, with your honor?"

"Yes, I will. Thank you. But I thought you didn't like magic. What changed?"

"You came," Selwik answered quietly. "All I know is that the magic has returned, and something is telling me that it is *true,* and somewhere inside I even remember what that means. I trust you, girl. I know you will keep the jewel safe and that, when the time is right, you will use it wisely."

"I don't know what to say, but thank you," replied Alannah. As young as she was, she felt a strange pride inside, golden and warm, like a secret that felt good. And then, she looked up at the door, and the blue butterfly was hovering on the lintel, again waiting for her. It reminded her that she had been gone from home for a long time and it was time to go.

After they closed the coffers and Selwik locked the door, the trolls led her back into the main chamber. They said their goodbyes, shyly and awkwardly hugging a little here and there, with promises of visits in the future. She turned to go when, suddenly, Selwik stopped her.

"What is your name, girl?" he asked gruffly.

"Alannah," she answered, and then she turned to leave, not seeing the sudden gleam that appeared in Selwik's eyes. She climbed the root stairway out of the tree to the surface and, as she climbed, she heard a faint hum of *aah* sounds and wondered at it, but now she needed to hurry.

She stepped out of the tree, and the blue butterfly led her back to the meadow and rested on a flower for a moment. From somewhere, perhaps in her own mind, Alannah heard, *Something long forgotten, a relic of long ago, a secret buried deep in the earth and old with magic.* And then, before her eyes, the butterfly disappeared.

After a baffled moment, she took the woods path home and stepped into her hut unseen. No one was there. She looked around, pulled out the loose stone she had found one day by the hearth, and slipped the box inside, wondering what the symbols meant and where the blue butterfly had gone.

8 Cloak of Innocence

Prince Tarek knew nothing of the hamlet girl Alannah, nor of the dragon or the trolls. His was a different world of courts and courtiers, one not as carefree as Alannah's, or as magical. As he watched and listened, he learned that the true power of the kingdom lay in the hands not of the king but of the king's advisors. These advisors smiled at the prince with all but their eyes, and showered him with gifts of toys and jewels. If they had stopped to get to know him, they would have understood that these gifts meant nothing to him at all.

Despite what he saw around him, as he grew older, he maintained his outward cloak of innocence, keeping his growing wisdom and knowledge hidden. One day, when Prince Tarek was about eleven years old, he was standing beside the king and queen in the royal attendance hall, listening and watching, as always.

Utrek, who was at the time the most powerful royal advisor in the kingdom, stood before the king with yet another manifesto to be signed. The king, as he put his pen to the parchment, just happened to look up then and see the question in Tarek's eyes, and he gave an almost imperceptible nod and then sighed before signing.

That day, at the end of the royal audience, when all but the king and queen and Tarek were left in the audience chamber, the king drew Tarek to him and clasped his shoulder. "My boy," he said, "I feel we have let you down. I was once, as a young lad, eager as you are, but nothing I did seemed to have any effect. I soon realized I had no power and I gave up trying. I have to admit, I am somewhat ashamed of that, and I'm tired.

"I am proud of you, my son," he continued. He looked away then, but not before Tarek could see the tears in his eyes. "I love you, you know," added the king, not accustomed to speaking thus. "I see your strength and your love for the people, and it is my hope that times will yet change under your rule." And with that, overcome with emotion, he left the chamber.

The queen stayed behind. She was silent at first, her love for Tarek pouring out of her eyes as she looked at him. She placed her hand on his cheek, gently cupping it, and said, "We both love you so much. You are precious to us.

"Do you know how blessed we felt when we were at last able to have a child, and to have that child be you, the light of our lives? You humble us, Tarek, with your sense of honor and right. We are in awe of who you are. No matter what else you think of us, know that we love you," she finished sadly. Before he could respond, she too walked out of the audience chamber.

Tarek realized then that his father knew the lay of the land and yet had not the courage to change it, or so he thought. His sadness was unbearable, and he felt more alone than ever. He began to walk out by himself in the forests and meadows of the kingdom, avoiding Rannulf as often as he could, yet still wearing the stable boy's clothes and slipping out when no one was looking.

It was then that he began to wish, more than anything, for someone to talk to, someone who could help him understand all that he saw around him. The land itself seemed to give him a sense of peace, but he still felt very much alone.

It rankled him that his father was so powerless. He began to feel bitter about him, blaming him for all that was wrong, especially the way the advisors funneled the gleanings of the land to their own coffers.

He stopped studying, except when in the company of his tutor. Before, he had loved the boundless exploration of learning, knowing he was helping his kingdom by doing so. Now, he didn't care. He didn't realize that what he was really feeling was a deep sadness, not just for his kingdom, but for himself too, for he was ashamed of his parents, and that feeling made him ashamed of himself.

And so, because he couldn't face that truth, he walked on the land and stayed to himself, as much as he could, all the while hurting inside.

9 Chocolate

Around the same time as the prince was feeling so unsettled, Alannah awoke from a dream with her belly churning. She felt unsettled too, as if something was about to happen, but she didn't know what it was. She wanted to tell her mother, but she thought she was too old for that now and kept her feelings to herself.

Lately, she couldn't seem to hold onto the peace and wonder of Dragon Meadow. There was a staleness and emptiness there, and a churning feeling of expectancy, of something unknown. Her body felt different too. She had become clumsy, as if she had two left feet that were too big for her steps. She kept falling over herself and couldn't even feel safe and happy walking in the woods anymore!

She didn't feel or see the faeries or nature spirits as she used to. It was different now. They seemed to be there but not there, visible only when her back was turned, as if they were waiting, watching—for what she didn't know. No one else saw them so she had begun to wonder if she was making them up. Her friends in the village school had made fun of what they called her imagination—her magic—so many times that she no longer mentioned what she saw or experienced. She had learned to keep it all to herself, secret.

Today, there was something different in the air. A feeling of suspense, of something about to happen, was beginning to gnaw at her, and she didn't know what to do or how to stop it.

She didn't know that what she needed was soothing and reassurance. So when she woke up irritable and cranky, she turned over to say something about the noise at the dry sink, and the sounds of the mixing and stirring of pots, and the clunking of wood being added to the fire.

But just then Anna, her mother, turned to her and smiled and said, "Good morning, my love. I have decided to make chocolate today because I have a feeling that somebody woke up in a not very happy mood and would like to be pampered a little. Am I right, little love?"

Now, Alannah was not so little any more, for she had grown tall for her age and was lithe and strong with her walks in the woods. Just now, though, her mother's loving words made her feel very small again, and she burst into tears, not knowing why.

"Oh, Mama," she said, "how did you know? I had a horrid dream, and I feel all strange and . . . thank you!"

She didn't say more because she couldn't. Her feelings were all tangled in knots of shapes and colors in her belly. It was enough that her mother knew something was wrong. *How lucky I am to have a mother like this,* she thought. And soon, the hut began to fill with the warm comforting smell of chocolate, and she felt better, knowing she was loved.

Chocolate was a rare treat for anyone, let alone a hamlet family. Recently, Jacob had done a great favor for the castle cook, delivering an extra load of wood at the last minute for a large banquet. As a thank you, she had slipped him a big chunk wrapped in oilcloth, telling him not to breathe a word!

As they waited for the chocolate to be ready, her mother sat down and patted her lap, saying, "Come, dear. Let me brush your hair. That always soothes you."

Alannah, with tears in her eyes but brightening a little, went to her mother and sat on her lap and allowed the touch and smell and feel of her mother to slowly bring her back to herself, and she relaxed.

With a sigh she closed her eyes and forgot her worries for a little while, and soon she was lulled almost to sleep.

The woodcutter Jacob tiptoed into the hut just then for his midday meal and looked at Anna, with a question in his eyes. She shrugged her shoulders, just barely, so as not to disturb Alannah. He gave her a look of such longing and fear that it brought tears to her eyes.

They had known this was not their own child, but they had loved her well. Anna knew what he felt. They both knew that, someday, their little girl would be the true princess of the land, and they were afraid she would forget them. They had kept the secret all this time because that was the agreement, but still, it caused them pain.

Alannah was his special little girl and had always been so. Every time he looked at her, his gentle love was filled with that same longing that he tried to hide, as he did now, when Alannah opened her eyes and smiled sleepily at him. "Hello, Papa," she said. "I didn't know you were here."

Jacob answered, "Yes, my child," cupping her cheek with his work-roughened hand. "I did not want to disturb you so I came in quietly."

"Oh, Papa," sighed Alannah. "You could never disturb me. I love you too much."

Jacob answered, "I love you too, my sweet girl. You enjoy your chocolate with your mama, and I will see you later. I must return to the woods now and chop some more wood." And with that, he took his pail and left, looking back one more time to wink at her and blow her a kiss.

When the chocolate was ready, Alannah slowly climbed off her mother's lap. Giggling like schoolgirls, they each took a big wooden spoonful of chocolate and sat down in front of the hearth fire to revel in the sweetness and goodness and warmth of the treat.

After a time, Alannah felt an urge to go to Dragon Meadow, and she thanked her mother with a kiss and a hug, donned her cloak, and walked through the hamlet smiling.

1 0 *A r e t e*

As she took the worn woods path, Alannah was still in part back with her mother, loving her so much and feeling so much better. But gradually, as she came to herself and noticed where she was, she noticed something else too. There seemed to be someone following her or walking alongside her a short distance away, and yet, every time she looked around, there was no one there.

The air felt different too. If it had a sound, it would be a soft whoosh. If there were something to look at, it would be cloaked in power. It was a vibrating, almost of the air itself. There was no crackle of twig or crush of leaf that alerted her. It was only the feeling in her bones. She began to tread more carefully, silently, as Dante had trained her to do when wary of strangers.

She continued following the path, but each time she sensed the thing, whatever it was, she stopped and looked around. Each time she felt a roundness in the air, a hovering nearby, and then it moved on. As she neared the meadow, she began to dread what she would find there, the feeling of whatever it was getting stronger and stronger.

Confused and bewildered, the chocolate forgotten, she was both pulled by the magnet of her curiosity and held back by the weight of her fear. Something was calling to her blood and to the pulse of her magic, yet it was stronger than her and very powerful. It scared her and fascinated her, willing her to continue on the path to Dragon Meadow.

When she got there, she did what usually calmed her. She ran and jumped and skipped and hopped, chasing the butterflies and the shadows of faeries, but it felt forced.

"Dante!" she called. "Dante!" She heard before she saw the beating of his great blue-black wings, as he descended to the meadow and landed just before her.

This time, instead of bending his great neck down in greeting, to be kissed and to share his heart with her as he had done since they first met, he stood at attention, solemn and still. She felt hurt and confused. Then he did bend his neck, but stiffly in a bow, and he seemed to look through her and then, she thought, behind her?

She quickly turned to look. There was no one there, but then . . . She could feel the presence of magic, but it was not like her magic that was innocent, free, light, and playful. This magic had intent, purpose, a sense of responsibility and weight to it. It made her feel uncertain and somewhat afraid.

As she continued to look, the air began to shimmer like a heat wave. It glowed and vibrated and slowly took form and solidified before her eyes. She was startled to see herself as a small child shape-shifting to herself now. It shifted again to what she might look like as a young woman and then middle-aged, all hovering through each other, barely giving her time to decipher what she was seeing before the shape shifted again.

Finally, the form settled itself into a lovely white-haired woman, tall, regal of bearing, beautiful, and graceful, smelling of roses, with flowers in her hair and shimmering silver robes, and a crystal wand of starlight.

The woman smiled as she said, "I am the white witch—the sorceress—Arete, pronounced 'AIR-it-tay.' I am who you have been and who you are becoming. I am your teacher in the ways of magic, as has been Dante, the Great Dragon. I have come to show you how to direct your magic, to use it so you may fulfill your destiny. It is time to learn who you truly are."

Something clicked inside Alannah, something right. It was as if all this time she had felt awkward and clumsy and incomplete was no more. At last, she belonged inside herself.

"No, my child. That is not true yet," clarified Arete, reading her thoughts. "You will still feel awkward and clumsy at times, but it is true that you have magic and that, when you have mastered the use of it, it will complete you. It is the place of belonging inside you, that is called *true*.

"There will come a day when you know in all of your being that you have come to the very moment of your destiny. And you will know exactly what it is you are meant to do. Do not fear this, dear child. Nothing can stop your destiny and nothing can stop your power, once taken. I am here to show you how to take it!

"We shall begin now. That is, if you are ready?" Arete said this as if there were no choice. Yet she laughed as she said it, knowing Alannah as she knew herself, for were they not one? One of past, one of future?

Alannah grinned, understanding. "Yes, I am ready. But what am I to call you?"

"You must not stand in awe of me. You must know me as the greatness that you will become in time. You may call me Arete, as that is the name I was given long ago in the time of the Great Darkness out of which I came. It will be your name also when you are in the times of your most powerful magic.

"Use my name to enhance your magic. Use my name to call it forth. Naming has great power. As does the written and the spoken word when it has intention. Beware of this, as you are aware of it, dear child. Know the power of a thing when it is said that 'it is spoken.'"

"Thank you," replied Alannah shyly. "I will try to remember all that you have told me."

"There is no trying to remember. There is only trying or remembering. I will be a fierce teacher to you, just as I will love you throughout. But mine is not a patient and petting nature. I expect greatness of you, as I expect it from myself, and you will see that I make few allowances. I will also pace our learning together so that you will not fall behind."

Alannah smiled widely now, even though she was still a little afraid. She was eager for this, hungry for it, as if she had been waiting all her young life for this moment. She stood taller and straighter, feeling some of the power that seemed to drip off of Arete.

"Good," declared Arete, smiling. "You have already begun. I see we understand each other. You shall start by learning to feel the magic," she added.

"But—" interrupted Alannah.

"Quiet now," said Arete. "You already have an inkling of what magic feels like. You have felt the *true*, have you not?"

"Yes, but—" Alannah interrupted again.

"Let me finish," said Arete firmly. "You must not interrupt me again, unless it is very important. What I was saying was that magic is like *true*. And without knowing what is *true*, you cannot have magic.

"*True* is when something feels completely right in all of your being, not the right or wrong that people talk about, but a rightness in your body.

"Experiment with this. Notice if there is any discomfort or hesitation in the moment. If it doesn't feel right, it isn't right. Trust yourself. You will learn to sense and use magic in the same way, by listening to yourself and listening to your body with all of your senses."

Arete placed her hands on Alannah's shoulders for a moment and then stood back. "Now you will really feel it."

"Now stand tall," she directed, "straight as you are and yet relaxed. Feet hip-distance apart, relaxed, arms hanging to your sides, relaxed. Yes, that's right," she said, as she did it too.

"Now, begin to feel the very center of you and the magic—your magic—that resides there. Do you feel it? Like a well that glows inside?"

Alannah nodded her head, her eyes round with wonder and awe.

"Now, intend that magic to enter your hands, your fingertips, as they hang by your sides. Slowly begin to raise your hands in a great circle, gathering more magic as you raise them to the sky, sweeping all in your field with magic. Raise your arms all the way up now and notice what you feel coming from above your head. See it. Feel it. Sense it.

"And then, when you are ready, tell me."

Alannah had always known she had magic, but now the magic began to pour out of her eyes and her fingertips, flooding the air all around her. As she raised her arms to the sky, it was as if a lightning bolt of electricity coursed through her veins from above, moving at the speed of light.

"Yes, that's it. And now, direct your palms outwards towards the sky, and see what you feel," directed Arete.

Alannah could feel an exchange of energy, of magic, between the trees, sky, and earth, and the magic that coursed from her hands. She was both taking it in and pouring it out, and the more she did it, the more it built.

She was startled that the lesson was so easy. And yet . . .

"That's right. It seems easy, doesn't it? And yet? Open your awareness even more."

Alannah did as Arete suggested, paying extra attention, and soon she noticed the earth humming beneath her feet, vibrating and pulsing as if it were alive. She could see the shadows of faeries and then the faeries themselves.

"Pay attention now," warned Arete.

Alannah saw the colors of the faeries' flights, like rainbows moving in slow motion. She saw the grass growing and flower petals unfolding, as she heard them grow and unfold, like the hushed sound of soft linens folding in upon themselves. She heard the words of songs in the breezes and the sighing of animals in the woods too far to hear with mortal ears.

And then she had a thought she immediately acted upon.

And Arete said gently, "Yes, go ahead and try it."

And Alannah began to pulse her hands in the air, as if the magic had physical substance and she was drawing it to her and sending it out. She watched the rainbows of it coming towards her and pouring out from her, like visible breath.

The grasses and flowers moved with it. The faeries rode in its current. She raised her arms up and the flowers rose up too and even uprooted themselves and began to flow in the current, bowing their heads to her. She could see their tiny smiles, and she thanked them and let them know she would take them home to her mother's hearth.

"Yes, it is good to remember that they are giving you their lives, as well as their homage, child."

Alannah looked to Dante now, and he was grinning his dragon grin with his great fangs showing, and his eyes were shiny with pride in her. He had been waiting for centuries for this moment. And now, he did bend his neck to her and, ever so slightly and gently, nudged her shoulder in approval. Then he rose back up again to let her continue the lesson.

Alannah dared to send her magic to him, curving her arms in a gesture of hugging him, as far away as he was, and yet she felt his scales and him feeling her hug, as if she were right there.

"That is because you have enlarged the force field of your magic to include you both. Good. You are a fast learner," praised Arete. "And now listen with all of your being."

And Alannah did, and what she heard was the sound of her magic. It was like putting a shell to her ear but louder. It was the song without sound, a song of pure joy. It was the song she was born with, and it was as if all had come full circle.

All that she experienced she described to Arete, although Arete already knew. "But as you speak it, you affirm it for all time, child. But know this now: You think that only you can hear the sound of your magic, but this is not so. Those of magic can also hear it, so now see what you can do."

Alannah, as though hearing the thoughts of the white witch in her mind, sent out her magic with even greater force than before, but commanded it, without words, to be silent, still feeling the joy in her heart. And then she looked up at Arete and laughed uncomfortably in embarrassment at what she could do.

For after all, she was only eleven and she was amazed at how much she knew!

Her magic did become silent, but she felt she had to confirm this, because she didn't trust herself to know for sure.

"Trust yourself," said Arete firmly. "That is a very important part of the lesson. And you must also take your magic seriously. You must show that you respect it and that you respect yourself. That is a part of what it is to be *true* inside.

"And you are right. I did not hear your magic that time, but this is what you must do.

"Close your eyes for a moment. Bring your arms back down the way they were when we started. Now feel with all of your being the well of your magic inside you. Know it. Strengthen it now. Even stronger. Do you feel it?"

Alannah nodded, solemn, silent, vibrating inside with excitement and wonder, but doing her best to hold that inside in the place of magic too.

"Good. Now do all that you just did but don't move. Do it all inside you."

Alannah stood still, and yet inside she was moving, somewhat differently, as her whim moved her differently, but the motion was as powerful, as strong, as colorful, and as magnetic as before! Afterwards, she opened her eyes and looked up at

Arete, and she couldn't help running to her and wrapping her arms around her in a big hug! "Oh! I'm sorry!" she cried, backing off. "I'm just so happy to know all this!"

"Please, do not be sorry," replied Arete, beaming kindly. "I am glad that you are happy.

"Now I want you to try it one more time, but this time open your eyes, look around nonchalantly, and walk a little while wielding your magic. And see what happens."

Arete watched with growing pride and love as the child walked in the meadow, with newfound grace and loveliness, sniffing flowers, looking to the sky and swinging about, all the while imperceptibly wielding rainbows of magic, the sounds of it turning on and off at her will.

Dante and Arete looked at each other. "This child is good," whispered Arete. "She shall do well," agreed the dragon. Even though Arete knew that Alannah would become a white witch—a sorceress—like herself, it had been a long time since she had taught such a one as her. They were both glad, for soon there would be a great need for Alannah's magic.

When Alannah was all done with this next exercise, she stood before Arete, hoping she had done well. Arete leaned over and hugged her, saying, "You were wonderful, my child."

Alannah beamed up at her. "Thank you," she said shyly. "It was fun!"

"Good. I want you to practice all that you learned today, wherever you are, whatever you are doing, until it feels like second nature, and then we will meet again. I will go now, but I look forward to your next lessons with great expectancy.

"I'm proud of you. You showed courage this morning when you followed the path, even though you could feel something, not knowing it was I who was following you.

"Before we meet again, it would be wise to notice if you feel any other energies of magic. Now I really must go. I have much to do on another plane. I will see you soon."

Kissing Alannah goodbye, she turned and quickly faded into a glow and then a glimmer, and then she was gone. In the glimmer, for one fragment of a moment, it seemed as if a blue butterfly hovered there, and then it too was gone. Afterwards, Alannah could not say for sure if she had even seen it.

"Goodbye!" called Alannah, sad now that Arete was gone, but also excited and proud of herself. "This is going to be fun!"

The moment she heard herself say this, she felt there was more than fun involved. She began to feel a weight of responsibility in the magic. She sighed, thoughtful for a moment. But then she ran her hands through the flowers and headed down the hill, focusing a moment to gather the flowers with her mind to take them, as promised, to her mother.

She turned back once to say goodbye to Dante. "Until next time," she cried. She watched him rise into the sky and fly off beyond the trees. She left for home in earnest then, thinking of magic and chocolate and imagining her mother's delight in the flowers that had offered themselves to her today.

11 The Faery Realm

Several months after Alannah's twelfth birthday, she was absentmindedly weaving her way through the forest, humming as usual, without really seeing where she was going, wandering inside her head even more than outside, to places she'd never been before.

She stumbled upon some roots, caught herself, and looked up, wondering where she might be. Thinking to go on, a small sound stopped her.

She'd heard the faeries laughing and giggling before. Their laughter was familiar to her, but here, added to that sound was the faintest shush of splashing water, so faint she wondered if it were merely part of her daydreaming too.

And oughtn't I to begin paying attention to where I am and how I'm going to get home in time for dinner? she thought. Of course, she could ask the faeries, but sometimes they played tricks on her and led her in the wrong direction, just for fun.

She looked around her, finding it unfamiliar, and yet as familiar as her great ones—those huge ancient trees—and her mosses and ferns and ledges and burls that peopled the forest, all of them friends to her. Before her was a great one she had not seen before, and growing at its base was a thicket of shrubs so dense she couldn't see through it. The sound came from inside this thicket.

She found herself circling the thicket to find a way in. She circled it once in one direction. She circled it a second time more slowly in the other direction. The third time, she closed her eyes and breathed deeply, allowing herself to feel her magic, allowing it now to build and gather within her, filling her heart and her entire being, more and more with each breath.

This time, as she circled the thicket surrounding the great one, she walked very, very slowly, each step a ritual, eyes still closed. She opened all of her senses and allowed herself to simply feel, just be, as the white witch—the sorceress—and the dragon had taught her.

There came a moment when it seemed that all the sounds of the forest stopped and the forest itself held its breath, and she knew this was the place. She opened her eyes, and she heard the forest sigh—she could swear it. Right before her eyes, the thicket parted like a curtain and held itself quivering for a moment, waiting for her to enter what she knew was a magic place inside.

She ducked to pass between the branches that stood open for her. Once she was through, the thicket closed behind her, looking as if it had never opened. She did not look back. She knew she was safe in the magic.

When she looked up, though, she gasped, for before her was the magical sparkling realm of the faeries. There stood a silver glass castle embedded with tiny sparkling jewels, tiny rainbow pennants flying at every turret. Tiny white marble sculptures of ancient faery kings and queens dotted mani-cured lawns surrounding reflection ponds filled with lilies. Hills and mountains, lakes and streams, wide-open vistas, and faeryland forests lay before her, all in miniature, even to the faery horses, goats and sheep.

Alannah could barely contain her excitement. It was like having a world of dolls come to life for her and yet, at the same time, it was her friends the faeries trusting her and letting her into their world. So many times, as she had been growing her magic, she had wished she could have known where and how they truly lived. Granted she was able to see them and hear them, but it was only in human surroundings. She had always wondered if the world of the faeries was really a part of her world, or did they have another, and now she knew!

The sound that she heard was the splashing of young faery children diving from big human-sized, dew-filled leaves on the edge of the thicket to smaller dew-filled leaves at the in-between-place, and landing in the faery reflection ponds. Then up they went into flight again, doing it over and over, laughing and giggling, flitting between the two worlds.

How Alannah wished she could move through the veils so easily. How she wished she could be like them. *Be patient,* she heard whispered in her ear. *Look already at what you can do, and see where you are in this moment. Be glad of this.*

She knew it was the white witch Arete and also herself who was speaking, that part of her that knew what was *true*.

I wish I could be small like them, she thought to herself, and the diving faeries looked up, saw her, and hovered in mid-flight, giggling and chattering to each other. She heard them call out in their tiny silvery voices, towards the silver-glass castle. And out came flying the faery queen herself, her wings moving fast as a hummingbird's until she lit upon a human-size leaf right beside Alannah.

She wore a silver-white dress spun of cobwebs sparkling with morning dew. Her hair was white and flowing like water down to her waist and a tiny jewel-encrusted crown circled her head. She was beautiful. She smiled kindly, saying, "I am Queen Esmerelda. Welcome to my kingdom. We have been waiting for you for centuries. Please join us."

The playing faeries too added to her invitation. "Join us!" they cried in their silvery voices. "Please join us!"

"Thank you for inviting me, but how is it that you have been waiting for me?" asked Alannah. "How do you know who I am?"

"Yours is the ancient blood of our realm," answered Queen Esmerelda. "I was there when you were thought into existence in this realm, into the human world. I was there at your birth, and I am your godmother.

"Do you not feel the stirring of your blood when you hear the tinkle of our laughter and the whirring of our wings around you?"

"Yes," replied Alannah, after thinking for a moment. "Yes. Sometimes, I feel you so close, it is as if I am part of you."

"And so you are, child. And so you are," trilled the queen, smiling and bowing her head slightly, as if in deference. "And we are proud that you have such a heritage. But come," she added, with a tinkle of laughter. "Now, you must join us!"

"But how?" asked Alannah. "I'm much too big."

"Wish it," said the faery queen, her beautiful voice warm and smooth as the finest pearl. "Wish it, just as you found your way into our world. Call in your magic. Use the power of your words, the power of your wishes. You don't have to try. Just wish it, and believe it will happen."

She smiled kindly at Alannah, and as she did so, Alannah did wish it with all her heart, feeling the kindness of the queen, feeling the eagerness of the playful faeries. She watched as the leaves around her began to grow bigger before her very eyes, as did the queen and the other faeries. And the castle grounds and the castle itself, and the faery fields and mountains and lakes and streams—all that was the faery world.

When she looked down at herself, she seemed to be the same size she always was, but everything around her had gotten bigger, and now she fit and she was glad. She was the same size as the faeries, and she squealed with delight, as the small child she once was. Around her all the faeries were laughing in their delight for her too.

Before she knew it, she had climbed to the top-most dew-filled leaf, and she stood on her tiptoes on its edge—as if on a platform before a flying trapeze. She held up her arms, took a deep breath, and dove out into the air, trusting, trusting, trusting, as she fell, that she would land in the water of the leaf below, and she did. Again, she tiptoed and leapt into the air flying and dove into the beautiful marble-lined pond of the castle grounds and, when she surfaced, those of the faery world clapped their hands and wings in applause for her joining them in their land.

She spent hours playing with them until even the youngest was too tired to go on. It was time to rest. Queen Esmerelda invited her to come into the castle for a royal tea, served by faery footmen in faery livery. The tea was made of honey and rosehips and raspberries, the best she had ever had. Each little cake was different, with pink and pale blue and yellow decorations made of spun honey.

Alannah was used to her mother's plain, good, healthy fare so this fancy royal tea was very new to her. She was delighted. Soon though, she stifled a yawn, covering her mouth as she was taught. The faery queen noted this and said, "I think it is time for you to go, my dear. We will see you again, if you like.

"Remember," she added, "all you have to do is wish it." Again, Alannah knew that this was *true.*

Esmerelda herself led Alannah to the place where the thicket opened, and it parted as it did before. But before Alannah went through, the queen stopped her.

"There is something I must impart to you," she whispered so that only Alannah could hear. "As I said before, words have power. Let me show you," and with that, she waved her tiny magic wand, and a window opened into another dimension. It was the dead cold of winter. Alannah saw the same leaves the faeries were just diving from, but the leaves were now dry and brown and brittle, and they were coated with a thin layer of ice.

A tiny shaft of sunlight filtered through the trees onto one ice-sheathed leaf. The ice began to melt and droplets of water formed. "You are so beautiful," whispered the faery queen to the first droplet as it fell. It formed a beautiful shape, like a multi-petaled flower, each petal intricately woven in white lace. Then it floated gently to the ground.

As the next one fell, Esmerelda whispered to it, "You wretched thing." The droplet formed itself into an ugly, misshapen thing. It faltered then plummeted heavily to the forest floor with a tiny thud.

"I'm so sorry. I love you," whispered the queen to the thing, and Alannah could feel the softening of the shape, as it melted into the earth, forgiving.

"At the very beginning of time," the queen told Alannah, "the Source of all things created the word *magic* and, out of that word, the dragon realm and the faery realm were born.

"Do you see what words can do? Do you see how powerful they can be?" asked Esmerelda.

"Yes," answered Alannah. "Very clearly. Thank you for showing me. Somehow, it feels very important to know this."

"Yes, and there's power in song too," she added. "Never underestimate the power of song and the power of joy." The queen was silent then, a silence that spoke almost more than her words. With a nod towards the part in the bushes and a wave to Alannah, she flitted back to her castle and was soon out of sight.

Alannah stepped through the parting and was in the forest then and back to her own size. She wandered home stumbling, lost in thought about all that she had just experienced.

When she arrived at her hut, it seemed that no time had passed. If it weren't for the fact that she had very little room in her belly for supper, she might have wondered if she had daydreamed the faery realm, and if it might not be real after all.

Alannah had a new place to visit now and new friends. She had a place to play and be very silly. She spent a lot of time with the faery queen who told her of the history of the land, of the land itself, and something about the people. She told Alannah how the ancestors of the human king had abused the land and not taken care of it, how the royal court had not understood about respecting the land and respecting each creature that lived upon it.

From her parents, especially her father, Alannah had learned to love and honor the land and all creatures. She was shocked to learn that everyone didn't care for the land as she did. She could not imagine anyone being but deeply connected to the land and all creatures. She asked Esmerelda many questions about this and stored what she learned inside. Somehow, she knew it was important and that, when the time was right, she would know what to do, just as the trolls had told her.

"And know, dear," tinkled the faery queen in her silvery voice, hearing her thoughts that day, "that when that time comes, we will be there with you too."

12 Different Lessons

As Alannah spent more time in the faery kingdom, she grew in experience and in her sense of self. She continued her lessons with Dante and Arete. Life continued to go on for Alannah in a very full and exciting way.

Just as she was learning and growing, so too was Tarek. Time was passing, and they were both fourteen now. Where Alannah's lessons centered mostly around magic, Tarek's focused on matters of state and court and country, old languages and dry mathematics. Often his teachers found him looking out the window, daydreaming, and they had to strike the desk with the royal yardstick to bring him back to attention.

He divided his days mostly into five activities. He spent part of the time with the royal advisors who droned on and on, filling their sentences with big words that said nothing, except to prove their own importance. He spent part of his time with the courtiers whose main goal was to gain royal attention to fill their own coffers.

He studied with his tutor. He practiced with Rannulf on the royal practice field—this part he enjoyed. He also learned the financial workings of the kingdom from the royal steward

Pander who was an old man and at least more down to earth, as he actually had a job to do for the money he earned.

Tarek took it all in, stored it for the time when he would be king, feeling a quiet sense of pride in himself for doing so and responsibility for the land and the people. Secretly, he guessed the advisors told the king the same stuff and nonsense they told Tarek, but the king, resigned, wouldn't admit he didn't understand, so he just signed whatever was in front of him.

Tarek was certain he would not do that when he was king. He already understood that what the royal advisors were saying was gibberish turned into sentences and paragraphs and meaningless mandates while, behind the scenes, they held all the power. He kept this to himself for now.

The courtiers bored him. He couldn't imagine having no interests other than coins, jewels, and stature, yet he smiled and appeared to listen and laugh at their jokes. He pretended interest in their intrigues and, again, kept his own counsel.

He listened to Pander attentively, both to what he said and didn't say. As he grew older, Tarek chose his questions discriminately, not wanting Pander or anyone else to guess in what direction his thoughts led.

Tarek continued to goad Rannulf to travel the land, to meet with the people and see for himself what conditions were like, and he went out by himself, as well. He learned more this way about his kingdom than any of those who spent their days in court.

Long before, as a child of eight, when he had begun exploring the castle, he had found a secret tunnel that led to a forgotten postern gate hidden by brambles near the castle midden. He continued to borrow clothes as he grew, and to sneak out through that gate without Rannulf's knowledge, so he could breathe in freedom and be by himself on the land.

Once off the castle grounds, he would wander to the foot of the mountain and along the edges of the great plain of wheat fields, where fieldworkers labored, keeping himself hidden just within the woods that bordered the fields. When he was tired of walking so close to the people nearby, he would seek the quiet and peace of the woods that seemed to befriend and harbor him.

Many times, he would simply sit at the base of a big tree, leaning up against it, and think—about his kingdom, his people, his family, sometimes about nothing. Always, he would come to asking himself, *Is there nothing more to life?*

He felt completely boxed in.

Sometimes, he couldn't bear the idea of being a powerless king like all the kings before him. Sometimes, he just wanted to run away and forget about ever being king. But then he would remind himself that he loved the people. He imagined what they would do if things continued as they were, and hoped he would indeed make a difference when he reigned.

He loved the land where he was born. At times, he loved it so much his heart almost broke, thinking of how the courtiers and advisors seemed to care nothing about it. He almost felt sorry for them in those moments, but then he reminded himself of who and what they were.

When he looked around the forest and saw the great trees, ferns, boulders, and shy creatures, he thought, *This is my place.*

When he encountered the people in the village, he thought, *These are my people. How is it I am so different from those of the castle? Why am I stuck there?*

Always, he ended up telling himself, *Maybe there is a way to change things when I am king. Maybe.*

13 *Alannah and the Prince*

ne day, lost in anger at the latest lies and courtly intrigues, and driven to wander aimlessly in the woods, Tarek thought he must be imagining it when he saw movement ahead of him. Immediately, he stopped and held himself still behind a tree, as Rannulf had taught him. Listening and watching intently, he slowly peered around to see a hamlet girl moving through the woods, almost silently except for her humming.

Just the fact that she was humming astounded him. That someone near the castle could be so happy! *What can she possibly be happy about?* he wondered. He had to find out.

"Wait!" he called out to her.

She paused for a moment and then walked faster.

"Wait!" he called again. "Please," he implored. "I just want to talk with you!"

Alannah couldn't help herself. She was who she was. She heard the pleading in the boy's voice, and her goodness made her stop and turn around to see a boy about her own age.

By this time, they were both fifteen. Of course, he was taller than her. He had dark brown eyes and brown hair, which was shoulder-length, and that was strange because all the village boys had . . .

Oh my goodness, she thought to herself. And then, *No, it can't be.* Then, as he got closer, she knew it was so, for all the royals had hair that length, and she had seen this boy in the royal processions.

"Oh my goodness," she said out loud this time, then dropped to the forest floor and knelt before him, saying, "Your Highness. I didn't know it was you. Please accept my deepest apologies. I had no idea. You are dressed so diff—"

"Please stop," said Tarek. Reaching out his hand to her, he added, "Please get up," and he pulled her to her feet. "Please, don't think of me as the prince. I just want to talk with you. You were humming, and I wanted to know how you could be so happy."

And then he looked at her, really looked: at the wavy golden hair that fell to her waist, her lithe healthy body, her deep grey eyes and the light that shone from them, and her sweet shy smile—and his heart faltered.

He didn't know what he was feeling. He only knew that, for the first time in his life, in the presence of another human being, his heart felt warm and glad and *true.* He wondered briefly where that word had come from, but then he realized she was looking at him also, and he forgot about it.

Alannah was staring at the prince. She felt prickly and hot, yet cold at the same time. She didn't understand it.

Her face went beet red, and she felt clumsy all of a sudden, which she hadn't felt for a long time, not since before she had started taking her magic seriously. *What's going on?* she wondered. *It must be because I'm in the royal presence of the prince.*

They were each so lost in their thoughts and feelings that neither of them actually seemed to notice the other, even though it was the other who prompted those thoughts and feelings! Finally, Tarek, practicing his princely taking-charge kind of role, as his tutor had taught him, cleared his throat, assumed a courtly posture, and came up with, "Er . . . ." He couldn't think of a thing to say after that, and his face turned beet red too!

Alannah looked up at him and then burst out laughing. For a split second, Tarek was shocked at her nerve before a royal presence, and then he burst out laughing too. Suddenly, everything was all right and they both started talking at once again.

"What are you doing in those clothes?" came out at the same time as, "How can you be so happy?" and then they both laughed again.

"Okay, you start," they said together, and then, "I'll be quiet," and, again together, "I give up!" Before they knew it, they were laughing so hard the tears were rolling down their cheeks until they had to hold their sides.

Then they just looked at each other and stood silently grinning, each hesitant to start. Finally, Tarek walked a few steps down the forest path, took a deep breath, turned around to face her and pointed at her, saying nothing.

She understood immediately, and began, "Your Highness, Prince Tarek."

He waved this away. "Please," he said. "Not here. Please just call me Tarek."

She didn't question him and continued, "How is it that you are here in the woods, dressed like a villager, and alone, without your attendants? What are you doing here?" They both breathed a sigh of relief that they had finally figured out how to have a conversation without talking at the same time.

Tarek explained about the castle and the courtiers, the royal advisors, the royal family—the royal everything—about his frustrations, and that he just had to get out of there sometimes. And then he ended, "But what about you? How can you be so happy?"

"I can't imagine ever not being happy," replied Alannah. "I have the woods and the creatures here, and the ferns and ledges and great ones."

"Who are the great ones?" asked Tarek.

"These beautiful old trees that have been here for so long and have such stories to tell. I love them all, the creatures, stones, ferns and trees, and I feel their love when I walk here. I even feel their love carrying me through my life wherever I go.

"I have my mother and father and the other villagers and—" (She almost included Dante and the white witch and the faeries, but something told her she couldn't speak of those things yet.) "And every day I learn so much more about all that I love. I have so much to be grateful for. How could I not be happy?"

The prince sighed. "I've never heard anyone talk about the things that are important to them, the way you do. I love the trees and the land and the people too, but I never realized they could love me back. There is so much I don't know, despite my tutors, advisors, and all that I have. Yet what I have means nothing to me, compared to all that you speak of.

"I envy you. I wish I could be more like you. You are free here. And I am in the prison of my birth. I wish there was something I could do to change all that is my world and make it more like yours."

Alannah kept silent. She looked at the ground, not seeing it, not sure what to say.

I've said too much, thought Tarek. *I was hoping she'd be my friend and I could learn from her, but I've said too much.*

He wishes for something different, Alannah was thinking. *He is wishing. Isn't that what I was doing almost right here where I met the faery queen? Was it meant that we meet here, at this spot? Should I show him? Dare I? I wish I could because he will be king some day, and I want him to see what I see, so he knows.*

Listen to your body, she heard. *From inside, from outside? What feels true?* she asked herself. And then, *How do I feel about showing him the faery kingdom?* Her heart seemed to well up with warmth and the tiniest bit of joy at the idea of showing the prince her world of possibilities.

It was only then that she looked up and really looked at him, right into his eyes. She sensed a sadness there and a longing for something he'd never encountered before. She knew what that something was. It was the magic she had inside her, that feeling of *true*. Suddenly, she knew he needed to find his own magic, and she could help him. Her heart flamed with joy. She knew that her helping the prince find his magic was one of the *truest* things she could do.

She knew he had goodness and wanted it for his kingdom—she had heard it whispered so in the hamlet where she lived—and she could see he was searching for answers for how to make it so. There began in her a tiny tingling that was the beginning of knowing why she was here, why she was born, and what the *true* was really about, and she was glad.

The prince had been watching her face all this time. Somehow, he knew she was not really looking at his outward self but at his *soul*. He didn't know where that word came from any more than he knew what it meant to know that it was *true,* but he knew he could trust those words, and he could trust her too.

Out of nowhere, he blurted, "I trust you."

His words startled her out of her thinking, and he saw her coming to a decision. "I trust you too, Your Highness. I don't know how or why, but I do. And I have decided—"

"Before we go any farther," interrupted the prince, "could you please not call me that? Could you please just call me by my name?"

Alannah looked startled for a moment, and then she smiled. It was like the sun shining in the forest. "Yes. I'm sorry. I forgot. If that is what you wish . . . Tarek. And my name is Alannah," she added shyly.

"Thank you, Alannah. Nice to meet you. Now, what were you going to say?"

"Well, Your Hi . . . I mean, Tarek. I thought that maybe I could show you something here that you might be meant to see," and she pointed at the dense thicket.

"Er," said Tarek again. "Well, alright, if you think so. I've seen a thicket before."

"No, I don't mean that," giggled Alannah, suddenly feeling shy again. *Why do I feel this way?* she wondered. "I think you are meant to see what is inside the thicket."

Tarek's eyes opened wide, as he looked around them. "But how do we get inside?"

"Please don't laugh at me right now. I know this may seem strange to you, but we 'wish' ourselves inside," she replied hesitantly, unsure of his response.

Tarek didn't know what to say. For the first time, he had an inkling of what his father must feel—stupid and ineffectual and blind. He must have missed something. Here was this beautiful girl telling him they could wish themselves inside a dense thicket. He wanted to believe her. She seemed sensible enough, so he decided he would.

"I don't know how we are going to do that, but I trust you," he said again. "You're the first person I've met who makes any sense to me and, just because this doesn't make sense, doesn't mean it doesn't. Does that make sense?"

And then he laughed at how flustered he was with her, and she laughed too, and they were all right again.

Then she changed. He didn't know how it happened. She looked exactly the same, and yet at the same time suddenly she seemed different. She became very still and took a deep breath. He watched as some unknown strength or power from deep inside her seemed to fill her and make her taller. She closed her eyes and said very calmly and very clearly, out loud for his benefit, "I wish to be inside."

Wondering what to expect, Tarek was astounded as a large section of the thicket seemed to move of its own accord, parting like a curtain. Alannah gestured to him to walk through in front of her. Taking a deep breath, Tarek stood taller to give himself courage, gulped and walked through. Alannah followed him, and then the thicket curtain closed behind them, hiding the opening completely.

Inside, he saw only part of what Alannah saw, for it was completely still. The tiny silver-glass castle was there, the tiny hills and mountains, lakes and rivers, sculptures and fountains and ponds, but it all looked like a frozen world of miniatures, lifeless, purposeless, and unreal. The prince was partially intrigued, but mostly disappointed. He had hoped Alannah had more to show him than a world of toys.

Alannah saw the disappointment in Tarek's face and wondered at it, for before her was the same lively noisy world of the faeries playing, flitting, dancing, and diving, and she wondered what was wrong. *Close your eyes,* she heard, and so she did. Then she saw what he did.

Without thinking, she reached over and put her hand on his shoulder. "Tarek," she said, the sadness and disappointment clear in his eyes, mirroring her own. "I am so sorry. I didn't know. I thought you could see what I do. I didn't know."

"But I do see it," said Tarek quietly. "I just thought you were different."

"No, Tarek, you don't. What you see is only the shell. I'm so sorry."

"What do you mean?" he asked. "What do you see?"

She told him about the faeries and what they were doing. She told him how she'd always seen faeries since she could remember and how she'd first found this place.

"Then, if I can't see them," said Tarek brokenly, "why am I even here?"

Listen, heard Alannah. The faery queen was right next to her ear. *Be patient.*

Can you not show him something? Alannah silently asked Queen Esmerelda.

Listen, she heard again. *Be patient.* This time she knew these words were not coming from the queen. They were coming from deep inside her, from her own magic, from all that she had learned so far.

So she repeated them to Tarek. "All that I know about this," she told him, "is that you are meant to see this much right now. The fact that you even were allowed here is an honor. Give yourself time. Stop and listen. Be patient, and in time you will be able to see what I see."

She stopped there. She realized that what she had just said was not entirely *true.* "Let me change that to, what you see may not be all that I see, but I was born different. I could teach you, if you want me to, so that what you see and sense and know can grow. But you have to want it. Do you?"

Tarek knew that it would help his kingdom if he could learn even some of the inner power that he saw in Alannah, as well as the ways of the faeries and the land itself. In that moment, he felt the weight of responsibility of his kingdom more than ever before, and he determined to take that responsibility as his own.

And so he answered gravely, "Yes, but we must keep this secret between us, and we can only meet in secret. I don't want any danger to come to you. If word got out that I was spending time with a villager, let alone what we were doing, your parents might find that you had disappeared without a trace forever. I could never let that happen to you."

Something blurry flashed before his eyes then, and it seemed that the miniature kingdom began to breathe. Without Alannah telling him, Tarek closed his eyes, stood perfectly still, and listened. He had the feeling—maybe he was imagining it—that there was barely audible cheering taking place somewhere, and he wondered, as he knew, that this was a beginning.

"And so it begins," whispered Dante, whispered Arete. All those who surrounded them in the place where they were nodded their heads in agreement, there on that other plane, in the ancient crystal cave of that *Long Ago* and *Far Away* beyond the mists of time. "The two have met at last. It has begun."

Tarek never forgot that day, or that practice of closing his eyes and listening within. It served him well in the courts and in his public dealings with the people, and it also helped to soothe his frustrations.

As it turned out, it was years before Alannah and Tarek met again, for as he was slipping back into the castle grounds that day, one of Utrek's spies spotted him. From that day, he was kept under a close watch, making it much more difficult for him to leave by himself undetected.

He wouldn't have minded for himself, but he feared for any commoners with whom he might associate, especially Alannah. He didn't trust Utrek and worried what would befall Alannah if Utrek learned that she and Tarek were friends. She, as well as her happiness, were both too precious to lose.

As the years went by, both Tarek and Alannah became busy in their own worlds, she with her magic and her family and her people, he with the royal court and his courtly duties.

Over time, the memory of that day faded for each of them as they went about their separate lives, although their hearts never forgot.

14   *The Crystal Cave*

Alannah was lying on her back in Dragon Meadow, hands behind her head, chewing on a blade of grass, staring at the sky on a sunny afternoon, daydreaming. She was eighteen now. She wasn't looking at anything in particular, other than the shapes in the clouds that she created with her thoughts.

She was shouting out loud to the meadow and the sky. "I love me! I love me! I love me!" she cried and then burst out laughing. She wished she knew what to do about whatever wasn't feeling right in the kingdom, but she didn't know, and that made her feel nervous.

She was being playful to change her mood. It was her way of taking care of herself. She was learning that, if she didn't love herself, she would lose her magic, and it felt good to do it consciously. It gave her a feeling of warmth in her heart, but also a feeling of rightness in her belly, that *true*.

The biggest part of her, the silent knowing part, knew there was a lot going on in the ethers, with the people and on the planet. She could feel it.

This knowledge came like wisps of smoke seeping into her being from some magical realm of "other" that she sensed was where *true* came from. It gave her teachings that penetrated to her core, initiations of magic that had no words or understanding yet, but that were important for her in some way.

She'd been thinking about how she woke this morning, feeling off center. Lately, she had noticed that, when she felt sad or anything less than *true*, she couldn't feel her magic. When that happened, she realized now, she needed to call it forth, out of her own deep silent well that was one with the wind, the stars, the trees and caves and tunnels.

She must trust that the magic was part of her, always. She must trust herself. She heard the word *true* whispered like a breeze in her ear, and she knew it was so.

She'd also been thinking that things felt different lately, outside of her. There was a feeling of sadness that had begun to color everything around her—in the woods, in all the beings of the kingdom, in such subtle ways that she expected no one else would even notice.

Whatever it was, it was growing and invasive, a great invisible dark cloud creeping silently and stealthily across the kingdom, seeping into every unguarded nook and seam in the hearts of every being. It seemed to have a smell that was not a smell, an aura of rottenness and decay.

She felt it so strongly now that she was impelled to see Arete and speak with her, without waiting for the white witch to come to her first, as had been the rule. The more she thought about Arete, wishing to see her, the more clearly and perfectly Arete seemed to appear in Alannah's mind.

Before she knew what had happened, Alannah found herself not in the meadow but in the woods. She had stumbled upon a ravine, which dug into a moss-covered hillside, tall trees on either side. Right in front of her was the mouth of a cave that was nestled in more roots, belonging to an ancient oak that stood hundreds of feet tall, towering above her. *Am I dreaming?* she wondered. *Did I fall asleep in the meadow?*

As silently as she could, she tiptoed to the cave's entrance and reached out a finger to touch the water that seeped down the moss that clothed the rock on either side. *I do feel this,* she thought. *I suppose it must be real.* And so she dared to tiptoe farther into the cave itself and, as she did, she could hear voices coming from the darkness.

The cave entrance reached just over her head, and its walls to either side were as wide as her arms outstretched. They too were covered with moss. As she went deeper into the cave, it grew so dark, she could barely see. Silently and stealthily, she crept in, feeling her way. And then suddenly, the cave opened up, and it was bright as day, with the light of hundreds of candles reflected in thousands of crystals and bouncing off the walls all around her.

She barely had time to take in the beauty of the place before she realized she must have stumbled into Arete's cave, uninvited. *"Is this a secret meeting? Is it even Arete's cave?"* she wondered, shrinking into the shadows behind her to hide.

Around a great standing stone of crystal-clear quartz, taller than a man, stood a circle of masters in long purple robes—masters she had never seen before but somehow recognized from a time long ago.

Among them were Dante, the Great Dragon, and many wizards and sorcerers from afar. They were all speaking at once, shouting to be heard over each other. "It is coming!" they were shouting indignantly in an effort to get the point across. "It is coming!"

Arete was there too. It was she who spoke. "It is here," she burst out coldly, angrily. "Do you not see it with your masters' eyes, or have you grown so accustomed to seeing the end— the all—that you can't see what is happening right now?"

All stared at her in silence, but Arete looked boldly around her, not backing down. Alannah wondered why Arete was so angry, and she wanted to reach out to her—her teacher, her mentor, her becoming friend—but she was afraid to draw attention to herself, for she was not, after all, invited.

Dante took up the cause then and roared in agreement. "It is *true* that the time is soon upon us when our little fledgling must act but—"

Here his voice made a sound almost of scales clashing harshly against each other and, if Alannah didn't know him better, for his great strength and power, she might have thought his voice was breaking. "—but will she be ready?" he continued. "Will she succeed, or will she be mown down in her innocence, in her love and tenderness towards all beings?

"We all know that what was written can be changed and re-written, according to the deeds of those involved. Even if one's purpose is written in the stars and the akashic records, it doesn't necessarily mean that the quest is completed in that lifetime.

"So, I ask again, what of our fledgling?"

"Is she ready?" asked Merlin, the greatest of magicians, and brother to Dante, the Great Dragon, in or out of form. "Is she ready?"

Alannah could hear them talking about her, and it filled her with dread. What was it she was meant to do? How could she be strong enough? How was it that all these masters and wizards and witches, and even Dante and Arete, were depending on her alone to do something that sounded so important and so terrifying at the same time? Starting to tremble, she closed her eyes and took a deep breath, willing herself to be strong. *All will be well*, she heard. She wondered who said it.

She placed her palm on her belly, bringing herself back into her body, as Arete had taught her. Then she brought her awareness back to the circle, out of herself now.

As she watched, a look passed between Arete and Merlin and Dante. Immediately, Alannah saw, like a transparency superimposed over the scene before her, a beautiful meadow resting in clouds, surrounded by stars and rainbows where three young children—two boys and a girl—chased each other in circles, laughing and shouting. They were at once human and, at the same time, luminous beings, their shapes shimmering and shifting into what they would become: Merlin, Arete, and Dante, the Great Dragon.

At times, they were solid, at other times translucent, or even rainbows. It came to Alannah that they were there to study the sacred texts of magic that they, as their ancient timeless selves, wrote long before time began. Sometimes, in their study, they tossed magic back and forth, as if they were playing ball. Or they held hands and whispered to each other.

And then, she noticed, near the edge of the meadow, there was one more little girl, humming to herself quietly. It looked like she was tending the broken wing of a mourning dove. Alannah heard the name *Iona,* but the scene faded and returned to the cave before she could learn more. She emitted a startled "Oh!" All those around the great crystal turned to look at her for the first time.

"So," said Merlin, "it seems her magic is so strong she is able to cloak it even from us!"

He looked around the cave, meeting the eyes of the other masters, a twinkle in his eyes. "How long have you been standing there, child?" he asked, turning to Alannah again, and looking at her with great tenderness. His voice was strong and clear as a still pool of water, yet it rippled silently in her head, like a mere whisper that lingered.

The look in her eyes gave him his answer, and he spoke for her, "Long enough, it seems." And then he cleared his throat and said more sternly, "You should not be here, child."

"I didn't mean to come," whispered Alannah self-consciously. "I just wanted to speak with Arete because I was feeling—" And she stopped, all eyes upon her.

Quietly, Dante sidled up to her. He bent his great neck down, gently nudged her shoulder, and said without sound, "What were you feeling, Alannah?"

She looked into his eyes, feeling safe with him.

And so, she began to tell them of the black cloud of sadness that was seeping into the pores of the kingdom. When she was done, the masters and wizards and sorcerers were nodding and whispering to each other, as if in validation of what she felt, and she was struck with dread to her very soul.

"You must speak of this to no one, child," said Merlin now, sternly but still kindly. "Do you understand?"

"Yes," she whispered, although she didn't, wishing she could disappear and make this not real.

"It is understandable that you feel this dread," soothed Merlin, "and yet already, child," he added kindly, as he peered around the circle, "you have learned the greatest of spells, and that is to trust the magic, as you trust yourself. There may come a time when you do not feel your magic, and you lose faith in yourself. You must believe in your light and in your magic, even if you don't feel it. Always. It is important that you remember this."

Alannah looked at him shyly, grateful for his kindness, and she smiled. There was now much talking amongst those standing around the central crystal and some arguing but, in this moment, Alannah was only aware of her heart and Merlin's eyes, for she knew she had gained another friend. It was as if she had known him for all eternity, and yet she had never seen him before now. *How is it that I know him so?* she wondered.

Just then, the group settled to silence and nodded to Merlin, giving him permission to speak. He said to her, "Child, it is time now for you to seek out the prince. Get to know him. He will be very important in the ruling of the kingdom and in its future. As will you be."

As before, a transparent scene, like a mirage, flashed before Alannah's eyes, a glimmer of a moment when a stream of magic flew and spiraled between two birth-beds—one at a castle, the other at a woodcutter's hut—and it put a question in her mind and on her lips that she did not speak.

Again, the scene returned her to the cave, but the questions were stirring something inside her, so she didn't at first hear what was said. Merlin's words about the prince hovered like magic curling around her ears until they finally registered, and then her face got hot, and her heartbeat quickened. She asked, "Must I seek out the prince? I am, after all, only a commoner! Must I?" She felt embarrassed. To be told to spend time with the prince! She in her peasants' clothes, and her feet that were too big, and her secret magic ways! He couldn't possibly want to spend time with her!

They had only met that one time, after all, even though they'd meant to meet again, but they'd both been too busy, hadn't they? He had his training in statesmanship, she supposed, and she had her training in magic to continue. Mostly, she'd begun to assume he didn't really like her after all, or why wouldn't he have sought her out?

It simply wasn't done for a commoner to seek out a royal. And now, they were so much older, and he'd grown so handsome and strong and . . . and, "It is just way too much!" she fumed to herself.

She didn't realize she'd spoken out loud. The annoyance in her voice woke her on her pallet by the hearth in her own hut. It was morning. *Was it all just a dream?* she wondered. But then, from out of her hair, fell a tiny bedraggled wildflower from Dragon Meadow, and she could see on the palms of her hands, traces of dried moss from the cave, so she knew it was *true* and of magic.

At the same moment, along the plain and up the mountain, Tarek woke up inside the midnight-blue curtains that surrounded his royal bed in the castle. He had had a strange dream about a crystal cave and the girl Alannah, and he smiled, faintly perplexed, then shrugged it off and went back to sleep.

15 *Arete Remembers*

A raven flew high in the sky croaking, circling, then landing heavily on the deep stone ledge of a narrow window built high in the circular, crenellated tower where Arete stood musing about what was to come.

"Spoke," she said to the raven, calling him by name. "What brings you? How did you find me?"

The raven was old, his feathers worn and ragged, for he had known many lifetimes and lived to tell many tales. He fixed one beady black eye on her, piercing her with a look that still made her shudder after all the years they had been friends, for she knew what he could see.

"I always know how to find you, witch, as you well know," he replied, chuckling to himself. "I just follow the path of the strongest magic, but today, I have to admit, I was blown off course by the child. It has indeed begun."

"Yes," she answered. "Alannah's power is greater than mine, even Dante's. I remember well..." And she drifted into thought, remembering the times of her own first learning and harnessing of magic, here in this tower room of spells and enchantment, crystals and incantations.

She remembered too her first human life among the cave dwellers, when magic was so young, it hadn't yet learned to hide. And other lifetimes, other places, where magic was as common as breathing, and still was on other planes.

Arete was from the Gypsy star system, known on some planes as Venus, where planets are created and star systems are orchestrated into form. Its archetype is the butterfly, for it is a place of transformation and change, and those from the Gypsy stars are shape-shifters likewise.

Who else's hand would have reached down from the heavens to scoop up and sculpt a stream of magic to shape the path of a princess and a woodcutter's boy? Who else would have thought to switch them at birth? Who else but the butterfly—gypsy, magician, shape shifter—flitting from place to place?

Arete was always moving, changing, shifting, her homes shifting with her, depending on her mood and the needs of her magic. Her home was a castle high on a mountain, a cave buried beneath moss-covered hills, a knoll of oaks and bluebells where the druids still performed their rituals, or a place in the clouds unseen by human eye. Yet all were one, straddling all realities, and she could be in all places at once.

The old raven too was from the Gypsy star system, as Dante was. Long ago, when they were first learning to build their powers of transmutation to create planets from nothingness, Spoke witnessed Arete's mistakes. The memories of that time still burned in her psyche, and she still cringed.

Shuddering, knowing he remembered even now, she said, trying to divert him, "There were few of us then, were there not? And we had so much to do."

"Yes, but you always had great power, as the child does. It just took you a while to understand how to use it so it did no harm, eh?" returned Spoke, turning his head to fix that eye again, glinting mischievously now.

"You always do that. You always remind me," replied Arete, embarrassed.

"Just keeping you in your place, mind you, so your head doesn't get too big!" he quipped chuckling to himself.

"As if I need reminders when you are around!" she laughed back, relaxing, remembering they were on the same side after all. "But getting back to the child, her magic is simple and loving, and it will speak to more of the people because of that."

"Yes, you are right," said Spoke.

"Don't you agree?" he asked, turning to Dante, as the scene shifted in a flash, and Arete and the raven were now deep inside the core of the mountain beneath her castle, in the dragon's lair that was also one of Arete's homes, and Spoke's as well.

It was a huge cave, the ceiling so far away that only darkness described it. The walls below glittered with crystals lit by the dragon's fire. A narrow channel of sunlight beamed down from the earth's surface to multiply like memories in the mirrors of the pools on all sides.

"Yes," chuckled the dragon, turning to Arete. "I remember well how you feared your power, and how the more you feared it, the more powerful it became, wreaking havoc along the way."

Immediately, there was a scene of mountains before them, towering high into the sky. Two great wizards taller than those mountains were flinging lightning bolts back and forth for fun, creating damage where they would and careless about it.

Their laughter rang across the sky, bouncing on clouds and reverberating and amplifying the sound until all that was heard was the earth-shattering laughter and the boom of accompanying thunder.

And then they were all back in the cave.

"Please, don't remind me!" cried Arete, mortified. "And what about Iona, our sister? Her curse wreaks havoc even now! At least I learned to harness my magic, but will she ever learn?

And then she added, wanting to change the subject away from her inadequacies, "Do you remember how in those days it was thought that the ascended masters were above us and all powerful, and we cowered like weaklings in their wake? It took us a long time to know differently, that we are all equal, did it not?" They all chuckled.

"This child is a natural with magic," she added. "She has known magic from her first breath and has learned to respect it. Love and joy are embedded in every facet of her being. That's why her magic is so strong. She still doubts herself, but that is to be expected. I have complete faith in her."

"Yes," Spoke and Dante spoke in unison. "As do we all."

Then Dante added, "It is written that she will succeed, and so we created her from the ethers so long ago. But we all know that circumstances can change what is written."

An uncomfortable silence followed.

Merlin appeared, with a worried look on his face. "Be wary," he said. "Even though you are down here beneath the earth, the land has ears. The combination of your magic is so powerful, all three of you, that I could find you easily, even though I was on the other side of the planet. Be wary. There are those, other than you, with powerful magic."

"I am surprised at you, Merlin," roared Dante quietly. "You never showed fear before."

"This is not fear, my friend," retorted Merlin. "This is about caution. There's a big difference. Iona's spell grows stronger daily. I would not put it past her to be able to hear us, even from here. Just be aware."

Dante and Arete shared a look but said nothing. Even Spoke had no retort. Finally, Merlin said, "We all know that all will be well, no matter what happens. But there is no harm in being cautious regardless, right, Brother?" He looked at Dante. "Sister?" He looked at Arete.

"You're right, Merl," they responded in unison. "We'll keep it in mind," added Arete, blowing them both kisses, and then they parted ways, Spoke sitting on her shoulder as she transported herself back to her castle tower again.

16 Jacob and Anna

Jacob, the woodcutter, and his wife Anna were simple folk. Jacob's parents both died of the fever when he was only five years old, so his grandmother raised him. As a boy, and then as a man, he was quiet and serious. He didn't play with the other boys, preferring to spend time alone outside, especially in the forest.

His grandmother noticed, loving him all the more for his quiet ways, treating him with kindness and respect. He said very little, but there was goodness in him and, when he did speak, it was always worth listening.

When he was ten years old, knowing she was aging, and that Jacob needed a trade, his grandmother spoke with Nathaniel, the village woodcutter, who felled the trees for firewood and cared for the forest. She asked if, perhaps, Jacob could apprentice with him, explaining how much he loved the forest, and what a good worker he was.

So Jacob began to work for Nathaniel, going out every day, early in the morning, swinging his supper pail as he walked. At first, he just stacked logs into the wagon that went to the hamlet and the castle both. But as he grew older and stronger,

Nathaniel taught him to choose the trees to fell, where and how to cut them and, eventually, Jacob came to know as much as his teacher. He loved the trees. He loved their gentle swaying and their silence, and the sense of peace they gave him. He often wondered what they had seen cross their paths.

Nathaniel was a widower whose wife had died in childbirth, delivering his only child Anna, who was the light of his life. At first, when Jacob started working with Nathaniel, she was too shy to even look at him. She was only nine years old, after all, and she had had little experience with boys of any age.

Slowly, over time, the two began to feel comfortable with each other, Jacob's growing respect and admiration for Nathaniel matching Anna's love for her father, and they became friends and grew to love each other. Eventually, when they were old enough, they married.

It was a great sadness for both of them that Anna never bore a child. They had each other, but still, each feeling the loss of parents and the absence of siblings as children, they both yearned to have a child of their own to love.

It was no wonder, then, that when the wise woman came to them and told them they would have a child after all, they were overjoyed and accepted the terms of their parentage. As Alannah grew from babe to little girl and young woman, their love for her and their pride in her grew also.

They had not known what to expect when the wise woman came to them, telling them of this child of magic who would do great things. Other than the wise woman, they alone of the people knew who Alannah truly was and, as she grew older and spent more time away from them, they began to sense the magnitude of her destiny, and they began to fear for her.

At first, when Alannah was small and spent her days outside, they were delighted, for she'd always come back with bright rosy cheeks and eyes full of excitement and love, and they knew she was happy. They also knew that the wise woman would protect her.

But lately, when she returned, just beneath the rose in her skin was a deathly pallor that spoke of something feared and, when she smiled, the smile did not reach her eyes. One day, soon after her visit to the crystal cave, about which Jacob and Anna knew nothing, they sat by the hearth talking about her, wondering what was to come.

Something was definitely wrong, but Alannah kept whatever it was to herself, and this worried them.

"What can we do to help her?" asked Anna, wringing her hands. "I love her so much, Jacob, and I feel so powerless. I worry that she will come to a terrible end, and I cannot imagine life without her!"

"Yes, I know, Anna," answered Jacob. "It is the same for me. But all we can do is love her and make sure she knows that. She will be queen some day, and we must let her go and hope she will not forget us."

"Oh, Jacob!" cried Anna, bursting into tears. "I cannot bear it! And we can say nothing to her!"

The two of them sat before the stone hearth in worn cane chairs crafted by Jacob, with soft cushions Anna made years ago. Jacob got up and moved across the hearth to crouch before Anna. He took his dear wife's face in his work roughened hands, tenderly as he often did at times like this, and said, "Anna, be still now. Alannah will be fine. You will see.

"Remember the wise woman who came to us at her birth. Alannah was gifted with a special purpose, and she would not have been so gifted if it was thought she would not succeed. Think of our girl's brightness and the joy she brings us. Think of the way the villagers look upon her and her kindness to everyone, including the animals.

"Remember that she has magic, and she is destined for great things. We cannot hold her back. We must let her go. We must give her our blessing."

"Oh, Jacob," replied Anna quietly, looking up at him. There were tears in her eyes, searching his, seeing the wisdom there. Somehow, it gave her a sense of peace. "How did you get so wise, Jaco?" she asked, using her pet name for him.

"Oh, you know, dearling," he responded in kind, a twinkle in his eyes. "I spend all my time around the great ones, the trees, and they tell me all they know! After all, they were here long before us, and even before many generations were even born! They do tell me things, you know!" he added, laughing at himself but, deep inside, he knew that what he said was true, even if he couldn't explain it.

"I am a simple man," he continued, "and you are a simple woman. It is not for us to question the purpose that Alannah was given at her birth. We must be grateful that she is in our lives at all, and that our dear son is being raised in the castle, even if we never see him." And this time, Anna saw the tears in his eyes before he looked down to hide them.

"It is as it must be," he added, clearing his throat as he stood up, getting ready to go. "Alannah has been as good as a son to me, when it comes to helping with the firewood. Come, Anna. We must be grateful for the blessings we have."

He reached down and patted her shoulder, and then he said, "I know it hurts, dearling, but we must be brave, for her sake. She must not know that we fear for her, yes?"

"Yes," agreed Anna, wearily. "You are right. We must show her our love and our support, and I will be strong, Jacob. I promise." And then she mustered herself and added bravely, "I have never heard you talk so much, Jaco! Are you changing in your old age?" And they both laughed, haltingly.

With that, Jacob stepped towards the door, and said, "I must go chop wood now. The days are getting colder early this year, and it looks like it will be a harsh winter."

"Yes," responded Anna, sadly. "You go now. I will be fine. You are a dear husband, Jacob, and a good friend. I wish you a good day."

"Thank you, my dear," returned Jacob. "Remember. All will be well." And with that he turned and left.

But as he walked along the dirt path through the hamlet and into the woods, he couldn't stop thinking of his girl, the daughter of his heart. There were tears in his eyes as he walked, as strong as he showed himself to Anna.

He wondered too what he would do if Alannah met her end in this mysterious purpose that the wise woman saw for her. And he was even more grateful that he would be spending the day with the great ones, the trees that brought him so much comfort. He always thanked them for their offerings of wood and only chopped down those trees that would help thin the forest, while making way for more growth.

There was a lot for him to grateful for, he reassured himself resolutely.

17 Lady Grove

From the day of the meeting in the crystal cave, in between cooking and cleaning, practicing her magic, and helping her father in the forest and her mother in the vegetable garden, Alannah searched for it everywhere she went. She thought she knew a lot about the land around her, but she realized she must know only a small part of it, for she could not find the cave.

Whenever she tried, she'd start at Dragon Meadow. From there, she'd explore each spoke of land that went out from the central hub of the meadow, and still she had not found it.

She wondered if she'd dreamt it after all, or if the entry to the cave was secreted away in magic. Once, she found a ravine that dug through a mossy hill, and she followed it to its end, to a rock wall there, but there was no opening in the rock. No matter how she stood in stillness, attending her center—her magic—no opening appeared.

She continued looking, over many weeks and months, and eventually her memory of the cave faded. More and more, the prince, and only the prince, held her thoughts.

She had still not sought him out, as Merlin had directed, but maybe it was only a dream after all, and maybe she didn't have to, or so she told herself.

Time passed, and she continued to put aside Merlin's directive, for she could not enter the castle grounds without permission, nor was she inclined to do so. Yet somehow, she felt linked to the prince, feeling a sense of destiny with him.

She was twenty now. Time was strange. Days passed like centuries, and weeks, like minutes. Her magic was more important to her than anything. She sensed that she must practice and hone it further, because the need was coming for her to use it, for the people, for the land, for the good of all. She had not found the crystal cave, and so she trusted finally that she was not meant to find it yet, but still the imminence of what was coming, and the growing sadness she felt in the land, kept her resolute and focused.

One day, practicing her magic, as she often did when walking in the woods, she came upon a little stream that wound and curled its way amongst the trees, gurgling and whispering in its own secret language. She forgot herself and followed it, held captive by its presence.

The stream curled its way deeper and deeper into the woods and began to etch itself along a mountain path that grew steeper as it wound its way up until even Alannah, as young as she was, and who spent so much time walking, was panting for breath.

Finally, the stream led her to a grassy knoll of land surrounded and hidden by great ones on three sides—thousand-year-old oaks—whose branches sang in the breezes above her. The sunlight shimmered through the trees, softening and dappling the long green grasses lining the grove. It was as if an ancient race of giants once lived here, who had sculpted this gently hollowed bowl of land. It seemed to have been waiting silently, patiently, all this time for the animal of her soul—the planet's soul—to curl up and rest here.

As she entered what felt like a sacred grove, Alannah heard whispering in her ear, *Wait, watch, listen.* She walked to the center of the grove and stood in stillness and listened again with her inner ears. Again, she heard, *Wait, watch, listen,* but no one was there.

She then paced the complete circle of the grove in one direction, and then the other, as was the rule of ritual, and still she saw nothing that might speak thus. And then she made one more circle with her eyes closed. This time, she began to feel, sense, see a form buried in leaves and moss, branches and stone. Eyes still closed, she slowly walked toward where she felt it, allowing all of her senses to open even further. When her senses stopped speaking to her, she stopped walking and opened her eyes.

Before her were branches and leaves and vines, just as there were all around the grove, but here, in this part, she felt that they hid something, drawing her to it. She began to gently pull away the branches first, and then the vines, thanking the mother vine for its offering. The more she pulled away, the more a form began to take shape. Finally, the branches and vines gone, all that was left was a great oval standing stone covered in lichen.

For some reason, she didn't know why, she rested her forehead upon its surface. Immediately, she felt the presence of the stone itself. She saw a great stone statue of a woman and, flowing out of her, came a love so full and gentle and embracing that Alannah was brought to tears.

The part of her that was *true* knew it was her own ancient self who wept for joy in this reunion. She allowed herself to simply rest in this stance, in this gently hollowed scoop of land, until she remembered herself and the image of the stone woman.

She opened her eyes. She stepped back, looking up, until she could see the fullness of the form itself before her, a stone six feet across and ten feet high. It was an ancient statue of a woman, her every feature blurred and softened by time, and wrapped in moss.

Barely discernible breasts, legs that met in a triangle, eyes and nose worn almost shapeless, and a face. What a face— even now, filled with love, after all the ravishing of time and the elements, and all that it had seen.

Alannah's eyes widened with awe. This was surely an ancient goddess of the times of the first people! *They called me Lady of the Earth,* she heard. *Wait, watch, listen. And sleep now. Sleep now.*

Alannah was so moved that she couldn't imagine sleeping, but she willed herself to do as the Lady asked. Dropping down at the base of the statue, she nestled in the long grasses and soon fell asleep.

At first, she dreamt of the prince and her dragon and her walks in the woods—familiar things—and then the dream shifted. She was in the oak grove again, but now it was night. The moon was full, and there was a luminous faery ring around it, tinged the color of blood. The stars were dim but still faintly visible.

The Lady, the goddess, was bright with moonlight, and she was alive and breathing. The stone of her mouth bent slowly into a smile, as her eyes shone with the piercing light of the full moon low in the sky.

Alannah in the dream began to hear faint chanting that grew like a wave until it filled the grove. Slowly, there appeared a shimmering presence of form taking shape from the mist. It wavered and then solidified into an ancient druid—long grey robes, long hair, long beard, wielding a torch.

And then another appeared in the same fashion, and another and another, until there was a ring of them that mirrored the ring of the moon and the circle of the shrine, all chanting in unison in an ancient language that the sleeping Alannah recognized.

The great stone neck of the goddess bent slightly down. Her head turned from left to right, as she watched the chanting druids step, one foot before the other in solemn procession. Her head rose then to look beyond the circle to the fourth side of the grove, to a mighty ledge that looked across all the land, the mountains, and forests, as far as the eye could see.

Below, halfway down the mountain, Alannah saw what might be Dragon Meadow. Farther down, she saw the young woman she had become, standing at the edge of a vast plain. The villagers were gathered behind her, and animals and peasants and workers of the land and the castle, all facing an army of beings so misshapen that, even in her dream, her body shook in terror.

They walked on two legs, like humans, but there the resemblance stopped. They had extra arms, or extra eyes or beaks or scales, or fangs that grew from faces that were lopsided and tortured and cruelly scarred, with skin the color of death and decay. They bristled with a power that was not of her world.

And yet, she alone stood before them, as if it were up to her to do something about them. Through the terror and through the horror, Alannah's dream self felt the touch of a living hand on her heart. And from that hand poured a warmth of love so steady and so *true* that somehow she was comforted and found courage to wait and watch and listen still.

One of the beasts seemed to move closer and, as she watched it, it became a mere glimmer of itself pulsing in and out of form. She could see through it to a scene of a man standing at his young wife's childbed. The man was wringing his hands in dire fear that she might die giving birth to their first babe, and the babe with her. Then the scene vanished, and the beast receded back into the horde of the army again. Through all of this, Alannah felt the golden love flowing through her, from the hand laid on her heart.

Her dream-eyes saw the Lady of the Earth as she once was, tall, resplendent, a great bulk of Mother, her face clearly sculpted. She wore a crown of branches and flowers. Garlands of flowers and vines and berries hung around her neck, draping her great bosom, an honor bestowed by the people of that time. Though the mouth of the lady did not move, Alannah heard, *All will be well. Listen to your heart. Hear what is true.*

Slowly Alannah awoke and sat up, blinking her eyes. This time, she did not wake by the hearth in her home. This time, she was still in the ancient grove, and the Lady statue was still there. From the Lady's eyes and from her great bulk, Alannah could feel the love pouring out of her that she felt in the dream, and she knew it was *true*. Alannah stood up and walked to the Lady, placing her forehead and hands on the soft lichen-covered stone, and she said a silent thank you. She smiled sweetly, knowing that, in this moment, they were one.

Looking up at the sun hanging low in the sky, she knew it was time to find her way home. Before she went, though, she walked the path of the druids in the dream. She could feel traces of them there, as if she were walking amongst them and, silently, she sent them greeting.

Then, just to make sure, she walked the shallow bowl of the grove to the ledge where there were no trees. Sure enough, she could see far below, down the great mountain and across the forests to the mighty plain. The *true* of it both scared and comforted her because now, combined with her fear, was the love of the Lady whose hand had lain on her heart.

And so she left the Lady Grove and found the stream again and followed its curving way back down the mountain. Now it did not seem playful, for Alannah's mind was full of a dream horde and a pilgrimage of druids. And she asked herself, *What does the dream mean? It felt so real.*

For Arete had told her of spirit dreams—Alannah knew this was one—and she must pay attention. And she remembered the feeling of imminent danger spoken of in the crystal cave, and wondered when and what was to come.

18 *The Scribe*

Up in the castle, Prince Tarek sat up, startled, remembering part of his dream. Alannah was in danger. Even though they'd met only that one time, he'd never forgotten her. *What was the dream about?* he wondered. He couldn't remember anything but a lingering sense of danger and the sound of weapons clashing. His gut clenched and his heart raced, and then he remembered the day ahead of him.

Another boring day, he sighed and lay back down. *Maybe if I go back to sleep, I can dream about her again, but a good dream this time.* He smiled faintly, thinking of her. *There's got to be something more exciting in life than learning to be king.*

The doors to his chambers opened with the quiet click of smoothly oiled brass, as did all the knobs in the castle, thanks to his mother who ran the castle with perfect efficiency. "Good morning, Prince Tarek. Time to rise and shine!" said his valet. *That's way too much gusto,* thought the prince.

The blue brocade draperies slid open, the sunlight stabbed through Tarek's closed lids, and he groaned. "I don't want to get up. I don't want to sit in on another meeting. I don't want to know how many bushels and how many bags and how many cords and how many sheaves fill the royal storehouses. I don't want to listen to neighbors complaining about whose cow stepped into whose garden. I just don't care! I need a day off!" he complained angrily.

Tarek could hear himself whining and yet, underneath the whining, there was a deep yearning, a longing, to be the boy he once was, the boy—the prince—who cared. Where did that boy go? How had he so completely forgotten how much he loved his people and his land?

But what I do every day in the great receiving hall seems to have so little to do with the actual people, he thought to himself. *It was different when I was younger and didn't have to attend in the receiving hall every day, listening to gibberish. There has to be something else to being a prince.*

All this time he was thinking, his valet waited. His face showed no emotion—no impatience or irritation—but the prince knew him well, knew what he too was thinking: that they each must do what they were here to do.

"Oh, if you insist," said the prince and slowly slithered out of bed, raising his arms for Garfald to help him into his royal dressing gown.

He dressed, as usual. He had his breakfast, brought in to him on a silver plate with a silver lid, along with a silver tray, which carried the silver pot and silver mug for his hot chocolate, which was brought to him every morning, as usual.

It was all meticulously arranged in exactly the same position on the tray as yesterday and the day before. Always, it was the same breakfast: toast and jam and clotted cream and eggs and bacon and sausage. At the end, he was allowed one piece of chocolate, held to the side until he finished all of his breakfast—*like a small child,* he thought to himself, *which maybe after all I am acting like, but still*—and given to him on another small silver tray.

Of course, he did what he was told. He was the prince, after all, and all eyes were upon him. *Just once,* he thought. *Just once.* But what he could do with that "just once," even he didn't know, he was so used to the same old thing, every single day of his life—except that one time. He sighed again, remembering what felt now like a faded dream of a day in the woods, when he met that girl Alannah.

He suffered himself to be brushed and inspected, like a horse in the royal stables. The breakfast trays were whisked away by silent, efficient footmen. The doors to his chambers were held open, his valet bowing as he swept the prince through yet another day like all the others.

Tarek descended the stairs, using the stately step he had been taught by the dancing master. He held his shoulders straight back and his chin up, as again he had been taught, to show the bearing of a prince. He stepped slowly down the great wide castle stairs to the floor below—screaming inside, as loud as his lungs could silently scream. He continued on to the great receiving hall where his parents, King Heinrich and Queen Isobel, sat in their tall jewel-encrusted thrones, in exactly the same positions they sat every day of Tarek's memory.

He knelt on one knee in front of his father so the king could place a hand on Tarek's head in morning greeting, as happened exactly the same every day. He bent to the queen to kiss her cheek in morning greeting, as happened exactly the same as every other morning of his remembered life. And then he moved to his own smaller jewel-encrusted throne chair and sat down and waited to hear the petitioners, all the while bellowing inside to be released from this prison of his life.

Is there nothing more? he asked himself again. He was twenty now, and the king was hale and hearty. The kingdom was at peace with all of its neighbors. There was no threat that he knew of. *Is this the way I will spend my days until the king is old and grey and feeble and finally dies, and I too am old, or old compared to now?*

He was so lost in misery that he barely heard the petitioners, and the fact that no one seemed to care whether he heard or not would have aggravated him even further if he noticed. It was almost noon before he found himself absently walking the halls, trailed by his attendants past various chambers and smaller receiving halls and drawing rooms and ballrooms.

He was still so distracted that he didn't notice a commotion in the hall, until he practically bumped right into it. A crowd of courtiers and servants, and underservants in the background, all hovered around some disturbance hidden behind the crowd.

"How did he get in here? Whose is he anyway? Get him out of here!" Tarek heard. He asked the nearest underservant what the commotion was. The underservant immediately lowered his eyes, bowed deeply, and mumbled something like, "There's a mangy dog that somehow got into the castle, Your Highness." And he bowed and bowed again and ran off, like a frightened rabbit.

That never used to happen, when the people knew me, thought Tarek. And then he looked around and saw that the attention of all of his own attendants was on the crowd and the disturbance, and not on him. He glanced back again at the underservant now escaping through a door that went to one of the service stairwells. Tarek slowly backed up, eyes on his attendants, backed up some more, and tiptoed to the same stairwell and escaped too, through the same door.

Quietly, so as not to disturb or upset the fleeing underservant, he tiptoed down the stairwell, hid behind doors, around corners, and behind furniture, so as not to be seen by the steady flow of servants. He finally found his way to the outer door, which spilled him into a peach orchard in full blossom, sweet with the smell of it. It was not picking season, so no one was there.

He sighed with relief. He had had no idea it would be this easy! He took a deep breath and reveled in the delight of his freedom, the sweetness of the scent all around him, and the beautiful day before him. It was a long time since he had felt this happy.

He started to wonder where to go and, immediately, he thought of that other day, long ago, and that girl Alannah, and he wondered how he might find her again. She was the only one he had ever talked with who felt like she was—what had she called it? That word? Was it *true*? Yes.

He didn't know where he was in relation to the woods where he last found her, so he climbed one of the trees to get a better view. The higher he climbed, the freer he felt, and the greater relief at his escape.

Then he heard someone sneeze! He started and sat perfectly still. *Please, don't let me be caught,* he pleaded silently to the gods or whoever might be listening. *Please,* he implored. He stayed absolutely still and waited. Someone was moving stealthily through the orchard from tree to tree. The person stopped right beneath Tarek's tree. He held his breath, trying to shrink his tall height into nothingness, and he waited.

Below him was a young woman from one of the hamlets. He couldn't see the color of her hair, for it was tucked inside her kerchief. Tarek couldn't tell from above who she was, but something about her made him feel strange. It was a feeling he wasn't used to, like a long-forgotten song stirring in his heart.

Though the light didn't change, the sun felt warmer, and the air felt charged and alive and the color of warm honey-gold. *Snap out of it,* he told himself. *You're not making any sense,* but thinking that didn't stop the feeling he had.

He watched as she continued on stealthily, still stopping at each tree to watch and make sure no one saw her or followed her. When she was far enough away, he saw her profile, and he knew it was Alannah. Even though it had been six years since he'd seen her, he would know her anywhere.

What is she doing here? Is she in danger like in my dream? wondered the prince. It was against the law for a commoner to enter the castle grounds without permission. He slipped down the tree quietly and began to follow her.

He followed her to the same door into the castle that he'd come out of and up the same stairs, but then she went a different way. He was about to stop her to ask where she was going, but then he saw her face, and it stopped him cold. Her eyes stared blankly ahead, as if she were sleepwalking. He didn't want to startle her so he followed, as quietly as he could.

It was true that Alannah was drawn blindly through the castle. She woke so, this morning, and the invisible pull was so strong that she had tried to stop herself several times, knowing the danger of being thrown in the dungeon for breaking the laws against commoners entering the castle without permit. But it was to no avail. She barely knew who she was, her magic was so strong and insistent.

It led her and protected her as she made her way silently down long corridors, ducking into empty doorways, crouching behind wardrobes and couches and credenzas, the pull of what wanted to be found joining forces with her own magic, to ensure that she was not seen or stopped before she found it.

She was so entranced, she did not hear the prince following out of sight behind her. Unbeknownst to either of them, he too was wrapped in her magic, it was so strong.

She wove her way deeper into the castle, into its farthest memories and enchantment—as if it were alive—the magic becoming stronger as, corridor after corridor, stairwell after stairwell, she came at last to the ancient stone stairwell that wound its way to the highest and oldest tower of them all. She took hold of the handrail of rope, thick as her arm, and slowly began the last climb. The stone was musty with age and dust, and the centuries-old leavings of animals that had found their way in.

At the top of the stairs was an arched wooden door, blackened by time, with great black iron hinges. Without pausing, the magic strongest now—both hers and that of what drew her—she lifted the black iron latch and opened the door. Then she blinked, awake at last, astounded at what she saw.

Sitting on a high stool before a higher slanting desk, in front of one of the curved tower windows, was a tiny wizened gnome-like creature, his fingers ink-stained and crippled with years of writing, writing, writing.

His pen scribbled even now on an ivory-colored scroll of paper whose length fell to the floor, reached across the room, curled and wound and eddied around the tower's circumference, and then crossed and circled over itself again and again.

What do you write? she asked the scribe silently. He did not answer with words. Instead, he showed her in images and vignettes: *the people's worst fears.* There were endless rolls of parchment lists. Unrolled and unleashed, they could have wrapped themselves around the entire kingdom.

She saw how he heard the stories—in dreams, in whispering lips of women in the market, in ancient finger signs made against witchcraft, or in the breath of the night sky, the ripples of a pool, the flapping of a single beech leaf in winter.

The power of the words—spoken, written, whispered, breathed—swirled and spiraled and poured their secrets onto the parchment pages until the pages were so covered with words—every fragment of surface—that the magic of them spilled out the window and poured itself into form, out of the netherworld of the unseen, into reality.

Suddenly, her vision telescoped onto one section of one page, and she found herself in a familiar story. There was a young woman about to give birth, and her husband was standing by. The terror he felt was stark on his face, terror that he would lose his wife in childbed.

As his fear grew, behind appeared, first a shimmering oblong shadow, then what looked like arms and legs and a head of sorts, and then a twisted face and twisted features, a moan, a cry of pain so dire, the features twisted even more.

Alannah watched as it wavered in and out of solidity. Its eyes turned red, it grew fangs and long claws, its head was shaggy and misshapen, and it vibrated with the energy of fear itself. *This is the visible form of the man's fear!* thought Alannah, shocked to behold such. She remembered the scene at the Lady Grove, of the same husband, and the army hordes at the end of what she thought was a dream.

She watched, as in a reflection pool or a dream, other vignettes of the people's deepest fears. Other forms took shape, one after another, spilling off the parchment pages out the tower window, falling to earth onto a great empty barren plain of bleached bones. Death and dread. A decaying smell of sadness without end. She felt deathly afraid.

This is the sadness, realized Alannah. *All the stories. All the people. But why is this happening? No one knows,* she heard, *and no one sees and no one hears, except in dreams and outstretched fingers of magic seeking power.*

Alannah was stunned. She blinked her eyes in shock and stared into the space where all the scenes had taken place, for now the ancient tower room was empty, but for bird droppings and feathers on the dusty stone floor.

She closed her eyes and breathed deeply. She didn't know what else to do. Her own fear began to escape her, reeling up inside, but she stopped it, not wanting to add it to a parchment page. She looked around the room, seeing in her mind the creatures and the plain, and the scribe writing the people's fears.

What could she do?

She remembered her magic then, and she reminded herself of the *All will be well* of the Lady, but her magic felt like a tiny ember inside of her. She didn't see how it could possibly all be well, if what she just saw was real. And the place where her magic came from—the place where *true* came from—told her it was real indeed.

She heard a tiny scuffing noise behind her, and thinking it was a mouse, perhaps come to comfort her, she turned around before the prince had time to hide. The look in his eyes told her that he'd seen what she did.

She turned away from him then and burst into tears, covering her face with her hands, in desolation for the people, and in shame, because she didn't know what to do. The next thing she knew, his arms were around her, and she was crying on his shoulder.

"I'm sorry," she said, "but I don't know what I'm supposed to do. It makes me so sad and scared."

"I know," said the prince. "I was worried you might be in danger, but I am beginning to see that we all are." He was stunned, not only at the scenes, but also that her magic was so strong that even he could see them. He hadn't realized. *Who is she really?* he wondered, but mostly he felt compassion for her, and awe at her courage and the power of her magic.

Slowly, her sobs subsided. The prince handed her a fine white linen handkerchief, and she blew her nose, apologizing for that too. Then she looked up at him. The look in his eyes, and what she felt in her heart, astounded her.

He tenderly searched her face in wonder, his eyes travelling to hers. He cupped her head in his hands, holding her face gently and, before he knew it, without thinking, he was kissing her softly on the lips.

An electric shock of recognition passed between them, and they stepped back a little from each other, startled and, at the same time, complete. She felt new, like a princess waking from a hundred years' sleep, and he felt like he wore armor and rode a white charger.

Then, despite the scenes they'd just seen or maybe because of them, combined with the kiss, they both burst out laughing with the jumble of their feelings. There was joy and release, and relief to be in the reality of their own wake-time lives, knowing they weren't on the plain with those creatures. There was also some embarrassment, for they neither one knew what to say after the kiss. Yet neither of them felt alone any more, for they knew now they were at least friends.

They were silent then and just looked at each other, not sure what to say. Then they spoke. "We have to talk," came at the same time as, "That was terrible, wasn't it?" They burst out laughing again, but it was nervous laughter, because of the scenes, but mostly their kiss, for they were each very aware of the complexities of their different social stature.

"Alannah," said Tarek, feeling protective, "we must get you out of the castle without your being seen, now more than ever before. I don't want you questioned. I have a feeling you might be very important to the future of this kingdom, even though I don't know why or how. And anyway, there are other reasons I don't want you harmed."

He cleared his throat and looked away for a moment. He didn't know completely why he said the first thing, but he knew it was *true*.

He led her down the stairs and out the quickest way he could think of. She used her magic to disguise herself and make the passage easier. As they made one particular turn, he pulled her abruptly into a doorway and held her there gently. Before she could speak, he placed a finger over her mouth. "Sh-sh-sh-sh," he whispered softly, barely making a sound.

He pointed to a man walking down the hall towards them, stopping here and there to speak with various courtiers. Immediately, Alannah felt a chill go up her spine. She could feel the energy of the man, and it didn't feel good. "Who is he?" she whispered.

"Utrek." The prince whispered the one word, and then they continued to hide in the doorway until Utrek had passed. "Be careful of him. He's dangerous."

"Whew," whispered Alannah. "I see." With that, they continued out of the castle into the orchard and wound their way to the farthermost trees to avoid discovery.

Once she was safe, they quickly decided on a place and time to meet again, which would give them time to think. Then they parted. Tarek was glad to have regained his love for his kingdom and his people, for what he saw in the tower renewed his purpose. He was especially glad to be reunited with Alannah, and he was in wonder at his feelings for her.

Alannah was in wonder too about Tarek, but right now she was mostly disturbed by the scenes in the tower and considered who to approach first, Arete or Dante.

Both Alannah and the prince were tired, emotionally drained and, for the moment, wanting to be alone with their thoughts and feelings. Later, they wondered individually, and even later, together, why neither of them thought to ask, *Who IS the scribe, and where does that power come from?*

19 Snow Crystals

As soon as she could get away, after seeing the scribe in the tower, Alannah went to the crystal cave to see Arete. She knew how to get there now. It was not a way of human step or human direction or dimension, but a way of magic that found it, and she knew that now.

Again, the light of a thousand candles reflected in the crystals that lined the walls of the cave and grew up from its floor in breathtaking beauty. Again, the masters and wizards and magicians were there, as if they knew she was coming.

She told them what she saw in the tower, and they told her, "Yes, the time is upon us. It is nearly here." And again, "You must keep this secret."

"But why?" she asked. "Shouldn't the people know?"

"If you tell them, do you not think their fears will grow and, with them, the army hordes?"

"Yes," she agreed. "You are right. But what can I do to help? There must be something we can do."

Wait. Watch. Listen. Again, the Lady's words. Alannah looked up, startled. She didn't know if she heard these words in her head, or if the masters were speaking them out loud.

"Either way, it doesn't matter how you hear them," comforted Arete, knowing Alannah as herself. "You will know what to do when the time comes, be assured."

But Alannah was not comforted. She could feel the fear trying to seep into her heart and into her belly, and yet she had been told there was nothing she could do for now but wait, watch, and listen. She closed her eyes and gathered herself and called on the magic at her center. Then she took a deep breath, opened her eyes, and said, "I will do my best. I just wanted to let you know what I saw . . ."

And then somehow her magic abandoned her, and she whispered, "I wish it were just you here, Arete, instead of all of these masters and wizards and magicians. I just want to be alone with you. I just want you to tell me it's going to be okay, and I don't have to be the only one that's supposed to save everybody. I'm scared. I can't imagine having enough magic to conquer those army hordes, and I don't want all the people I know—my family and friends—to die! I'm sorry, but that's how I feel!"

"We are sorry too, child," said Merlin kindly, stepping forward from the circle and placing a hand on her shoulder. "We are not gathered here to intimidate you or to overwhelm you. And it is not our intention that you do this all alone, this that is coming. We will be right there with you.

"But the act itself must be yours alone, for in you is gathered all of the goodness of the planet, a distillation of its joy and love and hope. It is only through your act, yours alone, that all will come into alignment and the transformation will take place. We have utter faith in you. There is no stopping your destiny.

"But know this, child. You were given a special magic and a special purpose, derived from the very Source of all things, before you came onto this planet in this lifetime. And all that you are meant to do, you were chosen to do and were given this magic to do it.

"We know that you have assumed responsibility for the power of your magic as it grows. We have seen you do it. There are those who take their magic lightly." A flicker of grief moved across his face, so quickly that Alannah wondered if perhaps she imagined it. For a flashing moment, she saw the scene of the two little girls and the two boys in the meadow,, and she wondered.

"We do not mean to put so much pressure on you," continued Merlin. "In time, you will know more, but for now, simply know that the magic you carry was given to you for exactly this purpose, and you will know what to do when the time comes. That is why you must let yourself heed those words, *Wait. Watch. Listen.*

"Continue your practice with your magic, and live your life as it comes, but also trust yourself, trust the *true* in you, trust us, and trust your magic. Believe me, child. All will be well," he added. And with that, he smiled deeply into her eyes and into her heart, and she believed him. Looking between him and Arete, she at last felt comforted.

"There is one more thing I would tell you now, my dear," added Arete. "All witches, whether they are for the good of all or for themselves, carry wands that enhance their magic. For some, it becomes a crutch that they lean on too readily. For others, it is something of honor, to be earned, and those are the most powerful wands of all.

"When you really know yourself, trust yourself, and name yourself as one of the strongest magic that speaks for goodness and the people and the planet, then your own wand will appear to you, but not until then. When the time is right, it will present itself to you."

"Thank you," Alannah said quietly. "I understand, and I know that I have much to learn still, and I am ready to do so." With that, she reached out her hand to Arete, to touch her arm, said goodbye with her eyes, and left the cave.

For days, her mind was filled with the words spoken in the cave and her need to believe that, when the time came, she would know what to do. When she was afraid, she reminded herself of the Lady of the Earth and the loving hand on her heart, and she was soothed. She continued to practice her magic in the meadow and wherever she went. She continued to spend time with Dante and Arete, and her life went on.

She tried to meet with the prince, but he was busy with the affairs of the kingdom and, since their last meeting, it was even harder for him to get away. Along with helping her father with his wood, she had been busy with the planting and growing and harvesting that fed the hamlet and kept it alive, as well as supplying the royal table. Despite their plans, it was winter before Alannah saw the prince again.

Ever since the time in the tower, she dreamt of words, swirling and flying, filling her mind and turning back on themselves. She had a hard time sleeping and feeling at ease, now that she knew of the battle to come.

This morning, she had dreamt the words, *The dream froze the words on her lips and her steps in the snow, like wet dough stuck in the hair of her thoughts.* She didn't know what it meant, but it made her feel unsettled, as if she had forgotten something important, and yet she didn't know what it was.

The feeling of sadness in the kingdom had grown, and she wondered if only she saw it in the eyes and the faces of those around her. People seemed to be quieter, keeping more to themselves. No longer was the hamlet filled with laughter on the long winter nights when the families gathered for storytelling with the old ones by the fire. It felt to Alannah as if everyone around her was unsettled, yet no one spoke of it.

Trust yourself, she heard, when she doubted her feelings. *Trust the true inside of you.* She didn't know quite where the voice came from. It might have been Dante speaking silently to her, or Merlin, or Arete. Or it might have been the voice of her own wisdom. *Yes,* said the voice. *Allow that all are true.*

It was winter now, and the harvest was finished. Snow covered the ground. It was early morning, and Alannah was walking in the woods. The sun shone brightly through the trees, turning the ice-glazed branches and twigs into sparkling diamonds glittering in the sun. The path was strewn with broken icicles, splintered off the trees. The woods were punctuated with the staccato sounds of lone shards falling and icy branches clacking against each other in the intermittent winds.

The path she walked cut across an open field, the snow on either side glinting in the sun, sparkling with tiny crystals sprinkled over its surface. Out of the corner of her eye, it seemed that the crystals were rising up off the snow in a flurry, and spiraling and dancing around her, and following her. But when she went to look, there was nothing there, and they were back in their places.

Again and again, this happened, until finally she stopped, and said, "Look. Show me what you want me to see. Whatever it is, I want to see it," and then she walked on.

This time, when a flurry of snow crystals gathered itself up off the snowfield and whirled around her, she heard, like whispers on the wind, "Dread." "Fear." "Terror." "Wrong." "Grief." "Enemy." "Punishment." "Torture." "Destruction." And more, as if each crystal had ownership of one word, and as it passed, it whispered its word in her ear. Immediately, she was reminded of the long scroll of words in the tower of the scribe and what those words invoked.

"I hear you," she said, her head turned towards the right where the crystals sounded in her ear, not knowing why it was that the snow crystals were speaking to her like this. She felt a coldness in her heart that had nothing to do with the coldness of winter, nor the wind that howled around her.

Again, a flurry of crystals pulled itself up off the snow, and billowed and eddied and danced around her left ear this time, and the words were different. "Hope." "Joy." "Peace." "Happiness." "Secret." "Magic." "Light." "Luminous." "Mystery." "Gratitude." "Freedom."

She could feel the difference in the quality of the two eddies. An idea began to form in her mind. *What if, when the thoughts of the people contain joy or freedom or happiness or gratitude, or any of the other words in the second flurry, what if those created different kinds of forms? Not like the demon beasts but like angels and faeries and loving beings? Can the people create something beautiful too? And if so, who does this creating? Who creates the army hordes?*

And then, she remembered the faery queen, and what happened to the droplets of water, as she spoke to them. She wondered if words like "hope" and "joy," spoken aloud, could help dissolve the horrid thought forms of the people, if they would just learn to use them in that way, consciously.

The idea excited her, and she began to experiment with words and what they felt like, the words themselves and the quality of them.

As she walked, the snow continued to eddy around her, but she didn't notice. She was too busy thinking.

Then the flurries seemed to take on mass, and the wind picked up and pushed her. She stumbled, almost falling, and then looked up. She couldn't tell what she was seeing in front of her. It looked like a thin veil of mist, but it was only in one place in the forest, between two trees on the path.

Words have power, she heard. There was no one there. She looked at the veil before her. She thought of the faery realm and the faery queen who showed her the power of words on a droplet of water. *Words have power,* she heard again.

She felt the veil beckoning. She walked forward to go through it, but no matter how far she walked, the veil stayed in front of her. *Words have power,* she heard for the third time. And this time, she knew for certain that it was magic, for she knew that spells were often said in threes. She mustered her magic. She felt her center. She raised her etheric arms and said without sound, *Open.*

The veil disappeared, and standing before her was Queen Esmerelda, but she stood as tall as Alannah now. "I stand before you, because you have discovered a great and powerful secret," said the Queen. "You have seen it for yourself, the power of words. You have seen the magic in them.

"As I have said, at the very beginning of time, the Source of all things created the word *magic* and, out of that word, the Realms of Dragon and Faery came into being.

"It was the blood of Source itself that pulsed through the veins of physical beings for the first time in creation. That blood is your blood. That blood is the blood of the Source of all things, and embedded in it is the powerful word *magic*.

"You have seen this. But there is more. With every word you speak, you invoke. The castle scribe showed you one way in which words have power. The snow flurries showed you another. There will be a time when the people are ready to understand all this and, when that times comes, it will be you who will teach them."

And with that, the faery queen faded into nothingness, and faintly in the fading, Alannah heard, *And again, do not underestimate the power and the magic of song.* The veil disappeared, and it was just Alannah walking in the crystalline morning again, with much to think about.

lannah dreamt: *A little girl kneels in a meadow, cradling the wing of a mourning dove, and croons to it, humming gently. Other birds perch on her shoulders, and a fawn and baby rabbit stand alongside her, looking up into her face, trusting her.*

She seems lost in her own little world, oblivious to the other children playing there, two boys and a girl. They call to her, beckoning her to join them, but she doesn't hear them, so intent is she on healing the bird. Her hands radiate with golden light and warmth, and the dove coos softly, sleepily, soothed by her healing touch.

When she awoke, Alannah sought out Arete for answers.

"Do you remember," asked Arete, "how in the cave with all those masters and others, you felt afraid and unsure of your magic? Well, that is what happened to the little girl you saw in your dream."

She began to tell the story. "There was a time, on that other plane, when the girl in your dream was one of us. She was sister to Merlin and Dante and me, and her name is Iona. (It is no mistake that her name means island, for she is alone, is she not?) We played together and learned magic together, but each of us had our own strengths and weaknesses, as all do."

"Oh!" said Alannah. "So that's who Iona is. I have heard her name and seen her, magic-wise, but I knew nothing about her, and I wondered."

"Yes, we knew this," answered Arete. "But it was not time for you to know. It is now.

"Iona's strength was in healing. In those times, all were descended from the faery realm, which is the oldest realm in the universes. Her powers for healing grew, and the faeries saw this and wanted the pure, undiluted power of her magic to join their own. So they transformed her into a true faery, and she became one of the most powerful faeries of all times.

"She did much with her own magic, and that of plants and flowers, and evolved a whole system of natural healing, until the day she lost her magic."

"But how did it happen?" asked Alannah, curious and somewhat alarmed.

"She lost her center," replied Arete. "More and more, her life was about healing, doing, finding those who needed healing, to the point where she forgot about herself completely.

"It is important that we must care for and love ourselves, not just others. If the love and joy that fills your heart is not also directed to yourself—if there is no recharging it within yourself—eventually, giving it away will deplete you and leave you empty. Resentment begins to sweep in.

"We were taught this on the plane where we learned our magic. It was one of the very first rules of magic, in fact. But Iona got so involved in healing others that she forgot to care for and heal herself, until it was too late.

"She began to seem rushed and irritated and overwhelmed. Her magic began to dwindle and twist and change, for there was no room in her heart to create any more. She became frustrated and bitter and then lost it entirely.

"She kept repeating to herself, 'I can't do it any more. I've lost it. It's abandoned me.'

"The more she said it, the more it came true, but not the kind of *true* you and I know. We three—Merlin and Dante and I—heard her, but there was nothing we could do. She no longer listened to us. And that's how it began—with the words.

"Her magic was still so powerful that it could call forth the wind and thunder and lightning and darkness across the sky. The land began to lose its light, as she did. But she didn't notice all this happening at first. All she knew was that she had lost her magic for healing."

"But then how is it that the sun still comes out and the flowers still grow, if the land has lost its light?" asked Alannah, confused by what Arete was telling her.

"It was not the light of the sun, or the light for the crops, that the land lost. It began to lose its inner light, the light of the spirit, a light filled with hope and promise, love and well being. Remember, the land is a living being too, as we all are."

Arete continued, "The more Iona repeated 'I can't,' the more she believed it, until she wanted no one else to have magic either. This all took time, and her magic was still so powerful before it was completely gone that she cursed the land so that all such words and phrases, by their very utterance, created those misshapen, lost beings that you beheld in the tower.

"You know, Alannah, how you've learned to cloak your magic so that even those of magic can't see it?"

"Yes?" nodded Alannah.

"Well, Iona knew to do that also, and in such a way that none of us knew or saw it, until it was much too late for us to undo her curse. Unfortunately, she cloaked it from herself too. So, you see now where we are and what we are up against. Iona is lost to herself, and yet her curse remains. You are our only hope, for despite the magic that she had, as powerful as it was, and as powerful as her curse is across the land, yours is that much more powerful, dear child.

"From the moment of your creation, and in the very naming of you, and in the song that is the vibration of all that you are, all the forces of magic were gathered to create you. You have the ancient faery blood in your veins, and you know with all that you are what is *true*."

Alannah looked up at Arete, her face white and drawn with fear. "But—" she started to say.

"Yes, I know, dear," comforted Arete. "I know what I have said is alarming, but I have told you all this so you will learn

from it. You must not lose YOUR center! You must believe in your magic even when you don't feel it. You must love yourself and care for yourself, despite your fears.

"Do you see now why I told you?"

Alannah swallowed and took a moment to still herself. Then, taking a deep breath, she looked right into Arete's eyes, and she said, "I will not let you down. I will do my best."

"Good girl," answered Arete. "We are all proud of you. And remember something else too. When you feel your entire body riddled with fear, ask yourself, is it fear that you feel, or is it caution? Fear serves no purpose. Caution tells us to think before we act. Caution tells us that what we are about to do could be dangerous. To label the body's feelings as caution puts us in a stance of power. Remember this!

"Your body is a wise familiar. All witches have familiars, do they not?" asked Arete, laughing, but serious too. "Your body is your closest ally. Listen to it. It will not let you down.

"When the time comes, you will know what to do. And remember: you are not alone. It is no mistake that Iona was named after a small island. She insisted she do it all alone. You are not alone! All those same forces of magic that created you, also created the path of your outcome.

"Dante, and Merlin, and I, and the faeries, trolls, creatures of the forest, meadows, water, and air, as well as the people—all are on your side. All you need do is wait, watch, and listen, and all will be well."

Alannah sighed with relief. She could feel the *true* of those words. The fear had dissipated. And all she felt now was hope, and love for this wise teacher of hers.

"Thank you, Arete. Thank you."

21 *Iona's Cave*

The next day, Alannah was out walking in the forest, and her magic and her focus on Iona drew her to the entrance to Iona's cave, almost as easily as finding Arete's cave now. Alannah had been feeling sorry for Iona ever since Arete told her how Iona had lost her center.

Alannah hesitated at the entrance but knew that, to heal the land and undo the curse, she must muster her courage and meet her adversary. It didn't occur to her not to, and she had a feeling that it was the power of her own thoughts and feelings that had drawn her there too, and she was curious. *For no one is truly bad,* she told herself, to lessen her fear.

So she tiptoed inside and slowly made her way down the rough-hewn path and along the winding, stone corridors until she came to the great cavern room. There, she stood just at the edge of the room, looking in, not wanting to alert anyone to her presence until she knew more about what was there.

The cavern walls dripped with minerals, lit by an eerie red glow coming from deep inside a blood-red crystal taller than her head standing in the middle of the room. Next to the blood crystal stood an old, gnarled, bent woman stirring the contents of a huge black caldron, and cackling. Surrounding her on all sides were those beings from the words—the stories—of the people's fears that Alannah had seen in the scribe's tower.

"We're almost there, my beauties!" she crooned to those gathered there. "It's almost time! And then the kingdom is ours! Ours! Ours!" She cackled again and drew from the ethers a handful of words that said themselves out loud—"hatred," "spite," "stupidity," "sarcasm," "failure," "enemy"—and sprinkled the handful into the caldron, immediately conjuring up more misshapen beings, who took their places in the circle about the room.

"Yes, my pets! We are almost there!" she chortled to herself and then groaned, laying a hand on her back, "and I will be returned to my magic, and I will be young and beautiful again! They will see!"

Alannah knew she couldn't wait. She must do something now before even more of the dreaded creatures took form. *But what can I do?* she asked herself, and immediately, she heard, *Be true.* And she felt the presence of her own circle of support around her, and her heart filled with love for them. She girded herself with that love, stepped into the red light of the cavern, and allowed herself to be seen.

"What happened to you?" she asked immediately, not wanting to lose her courage. "What made you hate so much?"

The witch looked up at her, startled. For a brief moment, a look of longing filled her eyes. Then a shutter closed over them, and she sneered, "What are you doing here? How stupid can you be? I'll eat you for breakfast, stupid girl!"

"I just wanted to meet you," replied Alannah timidly. "I mean you no harm. I wanted to hear your story from you," she added simply. "Will you tell me?"

The witch just stared at her. Finally, she asked, "Why?"

"Because I don't believe you are bad," replied Alannah. "I don't believe it, not after all the healing you did. I don't think anyone is bad. I just think they forget their light, and they don't realize it. I think something happened to you. What was it?"

The witch was silent for a long time, her arm paused on the ladle in the caldron. She looked into Alannah's eyes. She looked around the room. She gazed down at the contents of the caldron and stirred it again, absently. Then, with a "harrumph," she made up her mind.

"Leave. Now," she said to her minions, and immediately, they scrambled out of the room. She stirred the caldron again, to give herself time, and then she looked up.

There was a faraway look in her eyes, as if she didn't see Alannah at all. Instead, Iona saw her own past. Alannah shared that vision, drifting through scenes that Iona and Arete had shared as girls before things changed.

"When I was a very young girl," Iona began, "I discovered magic in my hands. Not the kind of magic you know, something different. I wasn't interested in the magic my sister and brothers were learning. I wasn't drawn to it. It was the plants and flowers, and the animals that I was interested in. I found myself becoming the plant or flower I held in my hands and learning all about its healing properties from the inside.

"Animals seemed to sense my gifts and would come to me for healing and, somehow, I knew what to do. The faeries were drawn to me too, and the elementals—the element, the being of each plant—and they befriended me. I learned to speak their language.

"I loved what I did. I loved my life, healing the animals and learning from the plants and faeries, and teaching them. I loved how busy I was all the time!

"I felt so important, as if I mattered, and it seemed to me that what the others were learning was so much less. I kept more and more to myself, only wanting to be with my plants and flowers and animals and faeries.

"I thought I was happy, but then, one day, my healing magic didn't work the way I wanted it to. It didn't heal fast enough. I had too many animals to heal to take the time needed to do that specific healing that day. I felt rushed and impatient, and the more impatient I felt, the slower my magic came, and the less it worked.

"I got angry, and it began to happen more often. I began to lose my confidence, and there was no one I could turn to because no one understood my magic the way I did.

"One day, I was working on an especially stubborn wound of a little fawn who had come to me to heal his leg, which he had snagged on a pricker bush. Nothing I was doing was working, and so I muttered, 'oh, curses!' to myself. Suddenly the fawn turned into a little gnome-like creature, with a pen in his hand, looking at me expectantly.

"'Oh, curses again!' I said, and immediately, the creature had a scroll in his hand and the word 'curses' appeared on the scroll. A darkish little cloud hovered over the ground, shook itself, and took the form of an ugly little creature, although I didn't think it was particularly ugly since I still loved all creatures then.

"I began to experiment with horrible words—the more the better—and studying the people's deadly fears, and capturing them. I enjoyed that power and that magic, which seemed to be working for me, at least, since my healing powers weren't working any more.

"So you see how I got here." The witch gazed around the cavern, coming to herself, and then she looked at Alannah. She said angrily, "So, what was the point of that? And don't you dare feel sorry for me! I will get my power back!" A look of doubt flitted like a shadow across her face before she could hide it, and she called her minions back into the room, to reinforce her coming return to power.

"I just wanted to know," answered Alannah quietly. "I mean you no harm." She turned to leave but then stopped herself. "But, do you really *want* to keep creating these word-beings, Iona? Is that what you really want for yourself?"

No one had ever asked Iona this question, nor had she been called by her name for a long, long time. The sound of her name drew memories of happy times, playing in a meadow with her sister and brothers, and it made her wonder.

She looked into Alannah's eyes and said, her voice barely audible, "I see why they say you are so powerful." She was silent for a moment. "No, I suppose, I don't need to create any more creatures, but it's not up to me any more. The curse is in place. The people's fears come up, the creatures exist and keep multiplying, and there's nothing I can do about it." She sighed.

"Could . . . c-c-can I . . . ," Alannah stuttered. Dare she?

"Spit it out, girl," said Iona, disgruntled with herself for being so soft. "Just spit it out."

Alannah took a deep breath, gathered herself from inside, looked directly into Iona's eyes, and asked, "C-c-could I hug you goodbye?"

"What!" screamed Iona, immediately in a rage. "How dare you feel sorry for me! How dare you!"

Alannah took a step back and another deep breath and said, "I don't feel sorry for you! I don't! I hope the best for you, and I hope you feel better soon, and . . ." She hesitated, took another deep breath and added, "I just want to love you, because I know you're not bad." And then, her gaze fell to her feet, then up again, into Iona's face, hope in her eyes.

Iona's face shifted from rage to curiosity and, finally, to amusement. She chortled, "You're a stubborn thing, aren't you? Well, it can't do any harm. And it's always a good thing to be friends with your enemies, anyway!" With a scheming look in her eyes, she added, "But hurry up! I'm busy!"

Alannah reached for Iona and wrapped her arms around the old witch, startled at how frail she was under all of those black robes. "Goodbye," she whispered. "I wish you the best. Goodbye." And then, just before she let go, she added quickly, "I love you," and turned to walk out of the room.

Neither Alannah nor Iona noticed how, when Alannah said 'the best' and 'I love you,' and earlier, when she said 'not bad' and 'feel better,' some of the word-beings turned into puffs of black smoke and disappeared.

It was to little avail though, because the minute she turned the corner and was out of view, Iona muttered to herself, "You stupid witch. How could you fall for that? How could you fall for love again?"

And she began to stir the caldron more furiously than ever, muttering and incanting—the worst words she could think of—in revenge against her own stupidity. From the back of the circle, out of the shadows, Utrek stepped out to join her, and the sound of his laughter followed Alannah out of the cave.

Alannah's magic told her, with chills going up her spine, whose laughter it was and, with her etheric eyes, she saw him there, and her body turned deathly cold.

From that day, Iona worked her curses faster and harder than ever, in her rejection of the love she had felt for that one moment. No matter how many loving, kind words Alannah spoke out loud, it was not enough, and cold and darkness spread themselves across the land, animals and crops froze, and those in the crystal cave knew that they must act soon.

$\mathscr{22}$ D r a g o n   R o c k

Alannah was dreaming much more, now that the time to prove herself was coming close. The dreams were spirit dreams, all of them. She remembered from this morning's dream the words "dragon rock" and "three portals."

Her practice of magic with Dante and Arete had taught her that a portal was a gateway to another reality, one of magic and mystery.

All she could remember of the dream otherwise was a vague feeling of being in woods, with no clear idea of where. She was certain this was a spirit dream, a teaching dream, and so she went into the woods to learn more.

She set off early to find what might be called Dragon Rock. This time, she did not go to Dragon Meadow first but found herself deeply listening, as if still somewhat in the dream, allowing herself to follow the path that felt right to her in the moment, and it led her high up a mountain. She climbed ravines between massive crags of rock, searching for what felt right. The farther she climbed, the more sparse the trees became, and the more light came in from the weak sun that had been trying for days to burn through the fog and darkness that had taken over the land.

She followed a path that she had never taken before. Others might not have seen it as an obvious path, but in the way of her magic, she could sense it was there.

She came to a small tree that arched over the path, just barely over her head and, immediately, she heard the word *portal.* She ducked underneath it, thinking, *This is the first portal.* She could feel the energy of magic increase around her.

The path continued to draw her and, soon after, she came to a mass of gnarled black grapevines that curled and arched over the path. She had to stoop to step beneath it. Again, she heard the word *portal,* and she thought, *This is the second portal.* The magic was even stronger now.

She veered off that path suddenly and turned to the right. This new path was even steeper and narrowed to barely two feet wide, running along the top of a long spine of land and stone that climbed even higher, falling steeply to either side.

She followed where her senses led, listening deeply within. And then she came to a thick fallen tree that curved over the path, so low that she had to crawl through it, and she heard the word *portal* one last time.

This is the third portal, just as my dream said, she thought, the magic so strong now, she felt drenched with it. Still she moved forward, climbing up and up, until she came to a clearing near the top, from which she could see mountains in every direction through the bare winter trees.

Is this the right place? she wondered. *Let me see.* She looked around for a place to sit and tried one moss-covered stone that looked comfortable and sat there for a moment. But it wasn't right, so she moved on to another stone.

This is a good spot, she thought. *So peaceful.* And she sat and waited and listened, allowing herself simply to notice all that was around her.

She heard running water, the caw of a single crow, the throaty tchur of a woodpecker, a clear trill answering its mate across the land, a squirrel scolding to protect its young—all, her friends.

The thin sun lit the carpet of dead leaves.

The mountains to the east were deep blue against the sky.

Just being here and feeling this peace is enough, she thought to herself. *There is magic here.*

And she realized that it was her magic, the simple magic of being and attending to all that was around her.

A slight breeze ruffled the dry blond beech leaves that dotted the dark brown trunks of the winter trees. A squirrel hopped from fallen trunk to stone to ground to tree, searching for breakfast. "Hello, friend," she whispered.

She sighed, reveling in the peace that was all around her. *I am so blessed,* she thought. *Thank you. It has been such a long time since I've felt peace.*

It came to her that searching for Dragon Rock was more about listening to her inner voice, choosing the path that felt right, and finding peace, than about discovering more magic to use when the time was right. *My goodness,* she thought. *All is indeed well. I am rich with this place, with this peace.*

She looked up, and there was the blue butterfly, hovering on a small branch before her, its wings rising and falling gently and slowly, as if it were watching her.

"Hello," she said, smiling. "Hello, my friend," and with that the butterfly flitted off the branch, circled around her—as if to say hello back—and then drifted off into the woods, shimmering. Then it disappeared, but not before, just for a moment, it transformed into the hazy shape of a magic wand.

"*Hmm . . . ,*" whispered Alannah, startled, wondering at that same time as knowing that what she saw was real.

Then she thought of Dante and his timeless wisdom. He had watched and waited patiently for lifetimes. She knew something had happened inside, something important. There was a feeling of trusting herself and allowing what was to come, and she felt the peace of that too.

23 *Ancient Blood*

There had been freezing rain for days, as if the planet itself were dying and weeping. Now, added to the cold and darkness, there was a growing layer of ice across the land, and few ventured out, for fear of falling and hurting themselves.

The stores, already scarce, began to mold and rot, and starvation and sickness spread amongst the people. Many had lost all hope for survival.

Only the children, in their implacable innocence and daunting fearlessness of any injury, were brave enough to venture out, picking their ways carefully on the slippery ice fields. They wore sticks tied with rain-softened reeds to their rag-covered feet, to keep from sliding. They scavenged for nuts and grasses and shreds of old harvests, some even putting mud to their mouths to fill their empty bellies.

Alannah too ventured out, for the same reasons, to help the villagers who were home-bound, but also in search of answers, ways of magic or otherwise, to heal the land.

She too tied sticks to her skin shoes, crafted by her father, now worn thin by too many years without new ones. Because she had magic, she walked more easily, but she had to hide her magic still until she was out of view of the hamlet where she lived. For generations, the people had feared magic, and it was not time yet to show them the truth about it.

Again, she followed the words of that dream from weeks ago, drawn to finding Dragon Rock. Again, she went into the forest where the roots and fallen branches wove safe passage in the ice, and, again, she climbed high, determined to find answers, or at least a return to the peace from her constant worry about her people and her land. Sometimes, she slid on the ice-sheathed rocks, despite her magic, but she kept on going, driven by something stronger than herself.

As she climbed, the earth began to feel warmer and the ice became mere slush, then nonexistent. There was something else going on here, but she didn't know what.

She followed the gullies between great spines and crags of rock—petrified land of old—up and up, and then clambered on top of the spines themselves, climbing even higher and, as she did, it grew warmer still.

Her muscles ached, her calves and hamstrings cried out for her to stop, but she was determined to do something, anything to help the people and the land. Near what might be the top—although each time she thought this, there seemed to be a higher place ahead—the rain stopped completely. She sensed magic here that was not just hers. *Is this magic of another kind?* she wondered.

Alannah came to a clearing where the trees were mere saplings, and she was surprised to hear the crunch and crackle of dry winter leaves underfoot, where the rest of the land was soggy or slippery with wet and ice.

She came to the same moss-covered stone where she had sat days ago, and this too was dry now. She sat and offered herself to whatever was to come, closing her eyes and allowing herself to sink more deeply into this place. Slowly, there came to her a sense that she was not alone, that there was *other* there. There were the usual birds and squirrels venturing out, one by one, as they recognized her, but this was something else, a presence.

Finally, Alannah whispered, "What can I do to help you? I am your friend, whoever you are."

There was a slight trembling in the dry leaves around her, like a faint rattle, but there was no wind. She waited quietly, patiently. Then she opened her heart.

The ground began to tremble and shake and rock back and forth and then, suddenly, the forest floor began to heave and rise all around her, the land coming alive. Trees fell and smaller rocks tumbled, as she found her seat rising up into the air now too. She grabbed for anything to keep herself from falling.

She had experienced much of magic by now in her life, but the sight all around her astonished her.

In every direction, rising out of the heaving land and shaking off avalanches of smaller rocks and trees, came the great lumbering, blue-black bodies of dragons—no longer spines of mountains, but beasts now—their long, powerful necks and heads unfurling out of the rubble, rising into the sky. As if the mountains were coming alive all around her, the sleeping dragons shook themselves awake before her very eyes.

She recognized Dante among them, but this was not the Dante she knew. He was much more powerful and, at the same time, only one of many. The greatest of them of all, the blackest, the largest, and the most daunting, spoke.

"We are the ancient race," he told her, his language one she did not know, and yet she understood. She had spoken it long ago in another time, on another plane than this one. "This is where we have lived on this planet for centuries. Humans think we live in caves, but we show ourselves in whatever form you imagine."

"But so many of you!" cried Alannah, dumbfounded and delighted at the same time. "Why now? Why here?"

"Let me tell you who we really are," answered the Great Dragon, his voice booming across the sky.

His wings began to rise and fall slowly, mesmerizing her. As if in a dream, she drifted back in time to a place where many forms of magic gathered. There was a great meeting there, and she recognized herself there, as soul.

She drifted even farther back, and she was in a world of beings made of pure light. All was light. There was no need for language or thought or action other than light.

Before that, there was a vast darkness filled with a love so boundless and so profound that it took her breath away.

"We are the ancient race," she heard. "Your people's time on this planet, the planet's time itself, is short, compared to ours, for where we come from, there is no time.

"We are the direct descendants from the Source of all things, as you are, and we have seen much. Now we simply wait and watch, as the planet moves through her paces.

"We are here with you, child, at all times. That you should offer us your love and support is an entirely new and unexpected delight, though not entirely unexpected, for we have known you as one of us, long ago, before eternity.

"We wait here in silence. We are bound in physicality in these mountains, all mountains wherever you look. We are the ancient keepers of the land, bound to silence on this plane until such time as it is right for us to stir and work our magic. We exist on other planes, in other dimensions where our lives are full and busy." Alannah saw glimpses of those lives. "But it is here that we are bound to lie, as mountains, sleeping dragons, portals anchoring the magic of other realms to this planet.

"Your love has awakened us beforetimes, but also, even in our sleep, we are aware of what is going on, and we have a strong urge to heal through our magic, which is the most powerful and ancient magic of all.

"Despite our size, we are of the same race as the faery kingdom, our magic going all the way back to the beginning of time, the creation itself, when the Source of all things sought to multiply itself into all manner of beings so it would not be alone. It sought to learn and expand itself, and to expand its love also.

"We are of that first blood.

"Ours is that same Source's wisdom, love, magic, and power. Eventually, there came out of us and the faery realm, human descendants who were to try their hand at life, using intellect, emotion, relationship, and creativity to further the experience of all. Unfortunately, humanity's greed for power and lust for control emerged as the extremes that won over compassion, joy, and love for one another.

"All this was seen and meant by that which is the Source of all things, but we were cautioned to be still, not to intervene, because of the magnitude of our power. It was hoped that all this would play itself out, and that humanity would come in time to a place of the greatest evolution ever, that of having light and magic, but also loving discernment.

"For it is only in three-dimensionality that sensation, even beyond light, exists. It is only here where one can feel the wind on one's face, water on the skin, the physical expansion of joy in one's heart. It is only here that one can smell the sweetness of a rose or lilac in physicality, or hear the haunting cadence of a song.

"We watched sadly where the complexities of human interaction and emotion and ambition took the race and, again, it was meant that we not intervene. It was not our place.

"The faeries, as you know, are as powerful as we are, and they still live and thrive somewhat in their realm, doing what they can for the land. But the people have grown wary even of them and blind to them.

"It is known that faery magic has no impact where there is no belief.

"That is the sadness that drenches this kingdom, in this time now. Belief is gone. Hope is gone. It is only power and greed that now reign.

"Even though we cannot intervene, your love, Alannah, at such a time, has awakened us. Know that we are here, all around you. Know that your song reaches us, here in the mountains, even when we sleep. Know that our blood thrums beneath the surface of the land wherever you walk, wherever you are. Our magic walks with you, even though we may not act upon it."

"My song?" asked Alannah, startled. "What song?"

"The song that created you," replied the Great Dragon, "the song that you are in this weary time." And again, she was shown a glimpse of a place beyond the ethers, and yet it felt somehow familiar to her. She heard, without sound, *And she shall be called Alannah, for the sacred ah sound of the heart.*

"Do not fear this," said the Great Dragon, knowing her unspoken thoughts. "Do not fear your destiny. All will be well." Alannah was reminded of the words of Merlin in the cave. "The Source of all things will not abandon you," he added.

Dante, silent beside her all this time, looked her straight in the eye and nodded. "Remember this," he said. "It is *true.*"

"I will, Dante," answered Alannah. "I promise. Thank you." And then she looked all around her, at all the dragons, especially the Great Dragon, and she added, "I thank all of you. But how is it," she asked Dante now, "that you are allowed to spend time with me, while all these others sleep?"

He nodded, having expected her question. "You too have the ancient blood of the faery realm and the dragons. Even before the time when Merlin and Arete and Iona and I played with magic, as children, you and I delved in a magic even more ancient.

"But your time was not then. It is now.

"I have been permitted to teach you now, to remind you of the magic we shared and who you are—the magic that is you alone. I will always be your friend and protector, and I hereby swear to you my allegiance for all times." He bowed to her now, as he did when she was a child, and tears glistened in her eyes with love for him.

Satisfied with his answer, Alannah felt soothed and found herself growing sleepy and unable to keep her eyes open. She drifted into sleep, leaning into Dante's shoulder. It was not until morning that she woke beside the cold hearth in the woodcutter's hut, and she wondered, at the same time as she knew, that what she experienced with the dragons was *true.*

And as she woke, she heard, *We will rise again.*

Mountains were never the same for her again. But at least, the land seemed to be warmer and the rain had stopped, and spring was struggling to emerge, despite Iona's curse.

Perhaps the sleeping dragons allowed themselves to interfere a little, after all, thought Alannah.

24 "Princess"

Over that cold winter that seemed to take centuries and yet passed more quickly than the breath of a wasp, Alannah and the prince were meeting in secret. She was teaching him as much of magic as he could learn and understand—without his being born to it. And he was teaching her about the workings and ruling of the kingdom.

They had turned twenty-one that winter, and their friendship had grown with them. They wanted to know everything about each other. So she had told him of the battle that she had seen coming in the future. He told her who in the court could be trusted and who could not.

She had opened his eyes to loving his parents and forgiving them. He in turn had helped her gain more confidence in herself, from the overwhelming sense of respect and admiration he felt for her, telling her often how amazing she was.

Mostly, they met in the woods where the snow was easier to navigate. Now that it was somewhat spring, they met in the royal orchards or in the meadow, and this was one of those times. The wildflowers that should have been blooming by now were yet stunted and grey with the cold of Iona's curse.

As they came into the clearing, Tarek turned to Alannah, laughing at something she had just said. Then, he saw her eyes looking up, and he turned around. Blanching, he stepped back immediately.

Across the meadow was a mighty blue-black dragon as tall as the tallest trees. Tarek stepped back even more, his eyes questioning Alannah. She simply smiled up at the dragon and said cheerfully, "Hello, Dante! I've brought you Tarek at last! Dante, meet my friend, Prince Tarek. Tarek, my friend, Dante."

Tarek watched as the great dragon curved his neck to the ground, as if bowing, and looked directly into Tarek's eyes, saying, without sound, *Greetings, my prince. You are most welcome here.*

Tarek, not knowing what else to do, looked fleetingly at Alannah, then gulped once and bowed himself. "It is a pleasure to meet you, sir."

Would you care for a ride? he heard.

How could Tarek help but grin and nod yes? Who wouldn't want to ride a dragon, after all?

And so Alannah and the prince went for his first dragon ride and, of course, he saw more of his land and his people. He was overjoyed and breathless with the experience, as anyone would expect.

They spent a day of it, traversing the clouds and stars, and crossing over the countries that had already become familiar to Alannah. At day's end, he'd learned a lot more

about his kingdom, and he was grateful and tired. He was struck by how both the dragon and Alannah seemed to take it all in stride, as if it were an everyday occurrence, which was close to true.

The sun was setting when they returned to the meadow. They thanked Dante and then turned to head back to the castle. Before they left, though, Dante loosened one of his scales and dropped it to the ground, as a gift for Tarek and a token of their new alliance. Tarek tucked it in his belt and, bowing, thanked Dante. Then he and Alannah went on their way.

Nearing the castle, they passed an opening in the wall that led to the herb garden, where they heard voices coming from within. Neither Alannah nor the prince thought anything of it until someone insisted loudly, "Only the true princess has the magic to vanquish the hordes."

Tarek stopped abruptly and stormed into the garden. Alannah followed more slowly, not sure of what was to come, but worried. *What did it mean?* she wondered, purposefully not guessing.

Inside the garden, Merlin stood arguing with Arete, and they looked up together. Arete sighed. She looked to Merlin for his tacit approval, and he nodded his head, as she said, "It is time they were told."

"Yes, sister, it is," answered Merlin.

"What are you talking about?" cried Tarek. "Who is this true princess you are talking about? This is treason!"

"No," said Alannah quietly, taking his hand. "Listen," and she closed her eyes, guessing, and dreading what it would mean to Tarek and their friendship.

And so, Arete and Merlin between them told Tarek and Alannah the truth of their births and who they really were. Arete gently pulled Alannah's hair back from her left ear and showed the prince the mark of the butterfly that was there.

All this, they explained gently and patiently, but none of how they did it mattered. Tarek was beyond crestfallen. His confidence deserted him. He felt lost and angry.

He was silent for a long time after the telling. And then he looked at Alannah with such bleakness in his eyes that her heart physically hurt to see it.

"I don't know who I am now," he whispered. "You are the true heir to this kingdom. Why did I waste my time getting to know the people, learning statesmanship, and swordplay, and diplomacy, and all the other trappings of a ruler, if I was never meant to be one?"

But Merlin spoke now. "No one in the kingdom knows this, but you two. You are still prince in the eyes of the people and the court. Nothing has changed. The time will come when you will understand. Be assured that all will be well."

"But why am I even here? What is my life for? What does it even matter?" cried Tarek.

There was such pain in his eyes, such hopelessness, that Alannah could hardly bear it.

"There has to be a reason for this, Tarek," she said. "I know it! The people love you, and you love them."

"No! Don't feel sorry for me!" He jerked his hand from hers, just now noticing she was still holding it.

He looked at Merlin and Arete and said, "Nothing will ever be well again. I don't care. Just do what you want! I never had any say anyway!" With that, he turned and stomped out of the garden into the castle, the only home he'd ever known.

"But what did you want to show me?" cried Alannah, just now remembering. But it was too late. Tarek was already gone.

From that day on, he avoided Alannah. She tried to see him. She left notes in their secret place, in a hole in the stump of an old apple tree in the castle orchards. She tiptoed as far as she could into the castle, both the grounds and the building itself, trying to get him to meet her eyes, to no avail. He was too hurt and bewildered to look at her.

She kept hearing, *He needs time.*

So she went about the business of readying herself for the battle that was to come. She missed Tarek. She felt lonely without his company. She wished beyond all hope that he would stand by her side at the battle. She wanted him there, but there was nothing she could do but trust that, in time, he would heal and come to her again.

$\mathcal{25}$ *T a r e k*

Weeks passed. Too many of them to count. Tarek paced back and forth in his chambers, running his fingers through his hair in frustration, saying, "I'm a fool!" He was disgusted with himself. "I'm a complete fool!"

No matter how he tried to convince himself that he'd been wronged, that it wasn't fair that Alannah was to inherit the kingdom, he knew he was the one in the wrong. Yet he couldn't force himself to apologize. He couldn't figure himself out.

"Why can't I just swallow my pride and be happy for her? I'm better than this! I know I am! What's wrong with me?" he cried, so frustrated with himself that he started looking around for something to throw. His eyes lit on the dragon scale Dante had given him when he and Alannah were still talking. It was glowing, as if trying to tell him something, and the glow reminded him of Alannah, of who she was.

Suddenly, it dawned on him. Suddenly, he knew. He stood stock still, frozen in shock.

"I really love her," he whispered to himself, in awe. "All this time we've spent together, I thought we were just friends.

I knew we were, even though we kissed each other that one time in the tower. But I thought that was out of fear and relief and all that we'd seen.

"I've been feeling so betrayed, but she didn't know who she was either! How can I possibly blame her? Whatever happens, it's my path. Wherever it goes, it's right for me. I have to trust that, just the way she trusts.

"I love her!" he said again, jubilantly. Like a dimwit—or so he called himself later—he started dancing around the room with joy.

Then he stopped. Still.

"The darkness," he whispered. "The cold. Her magic. The battle. The little she's told me . . .

"She needs me by her side. I have to be there. I have to show her I love her, and I have to show the people I support her in all she does. She needs me there."

Tarek sighed in relief, and then he realized, "I have to go NOW. I have to go to where she lives, and tell her I'm sorry."

He'd never been to the woodcutter's hut before. He knew which hamlet it was, though, and he was sure he could find it. After all, he used to visit all the hamlets when he was younger and still hopeful of change.

It was dawn, and he hadn't been able to sleep all night. In truth, he hadn't been able to sleep very well for weeks, ever since he had learned of the true nature of his birth. Even though he was supposed to be meeting with the council today, and his tutor, and the castle steward, and all the others, he knew he had to act now. He tucked the dragon scale into his belt, grabbed his sword, slid it into its scabbard, and hurried out the castle through the midden gate. He went off at a run, loping his way down the mountain to Alannah's hamlet, hoping he wasn't too late.

This time, he didn't skirt the plain to avoid being seen. This time, he strode openly across the fields. He wanted the people to see him, to know that he was there, supporting Alannah all the way.

But he was not the only one headed there. Others were ahead of him, hurrying, from all directions.

Even before he got there, he could hear the crowd, the tumult, the voices. He saw the villagers on one side of the plain, carrying pikes and staffs and shovels, and animals in droves, and on the other side were startling hordes of ugly, misshapen creatures carrying weapons. He hadn't known the battle was today. Again, he hoped he wasn't too late, and he was glad he carried his sword.

Alannah needs me, he heard, and he knew it as *true.*

2 6 *All Through the Night*

All through the night, from all across the land, like a steady flow of rivulets and streams and rivers gathering strength as they descended, came the animals, silently, one by one, and then the people. No one could sleep, and no one knew why.

Although she had told no one but Tarek about the impending battle, the land knew. The land whispered into the sleeping psyches of its people and its creatures. It woke them and prodded them dream-wise to gather at the hamlet where Alannah lived. The faeries whispered too. What the people heard was, *Alannah needs us. Alannah needs us.*

From beyond the outlying hamlets, they came. Out of the woods and off the mountains, animals poured across the land, armed with claws, tusks, antlers, or fangs—foxes, boars, wolves, and badgers, bears, elk, coyotes, and mountain lions. Birds of prey—hawks, eagles, owls, and vultures—circled overhead, with claws and beaks and powerful wings.

The people followed. Those who tilled the fields of the great plain and worked the orchards, bearing hoes, shovels, rakes, and pitchforks. Shepherds and goatherds spilled from the hills, with their staffs and sling shots, and woodsmen and huntsmen with their axes and bows. Even the goose girls came with their sharp-beaked geese, and the weavers and spinners with needles and spindles.

Those of the orchards and herb gardens infiltrated the castle before they left and alerted the indoor servants, and they came too. The cooks with their heavy iron ladles, the cleaning women with their mops and brooms, the stable men with their whips, led by Rannulf. He did not know Alannah, but he'd heard of her from Tarek and felt the call and loved the land.

The trolls came, and the faeries, led by Queen Esmerelda. And the land shook as the sleeping dragons awoke again.

Word spread like wildfire to the outlying hamlets and hidden places where word seldom reached at all. It was these stragglers whom Tarek joined.

Across the other side of the plain, from off Iona's mountain and out of her cave, spilled the hordes of misshapen beings formed of the people's fears, and they too readied themselves for battle.

At midnight, Iona had sounded the alarm and raised her standard, and the march of the hordes had begun. They came like ants to sugar, tumbling over each other in their zeal to kill and maim and destroy. They were armed with bows and spears, battle-axes and swords, maces and mauls and clubs.

Wherever they tread, they left the land scarred and scorched and screaming silently in their wake.

When dawn came, the last stragglers were just arriving, and Tarek was with them. The wild animals were there, milling and pacing, the birds of the sky circling above. All stood in readiness: the people massed around and outside of Alannah's hamlet; and the great hordes across the plain at the base of Iona's mountain. They all waited for the signal.

They all waited for Alannah to appear.

And then, the door to the simple woodcutter's hut opened, and Alannah stepped out. Her face turned white with shock. She looked at all those gathered there, in the woods before her hut and as far as her eyes could see to the great plain. She firmed her stance and straightened her shoulders. Then, she strode forward, the crowd parting as she went, and took her place at the fore of her people, on the edge of the great plain, just as she'd seen in her dream at Lady Grove.

It was at that moment that Tarek arrived. His gut clenched in dread as he saw her taking that stand, as if she alone could protect them. His Alannah—standing tall and looking so strong! But when he looked closer, he could see her hands tremble and her face, white as a sheet. He could almost smell her fear.

He knew it was too late to stand next to her, because he didn't want to distract her, so he got as close as he could, threading his way through the crowd until he was just behind her. What mattered most was that he was there, and loved her and believed in her, and showed that to the people.

27 *The Battle*

That morning, Alannah had awoken as usual by the hearth, feeling an air of expectancy. She knew without being told that the great day was upon her, the day of the battle. She could smell it. She could feel it in the pit of her stomach, roiling like a viper's nest. She knew there was nothing she could do to avoid it.

Tarek was still not speaking to her. It was too late now to wish for him to be there, to wish for anything other than survival for herself and her people and the land.

She sighed, hating the feeling in her belly, so she closed her eyes and found the light inside, and she felt a little better.

She reached down beside her and loosened the stone that hid the box with her blue butterfly stone—the sapphire—and pulled it from its hiding place. This was the first time she had admitted to herself what it was, a priceless jewel owned by a mere hamlet girl. She knew she was born the princess, but she was still a hamlet girl inside. She hadn't wanted to think about its value before, and what she was doing with it, or why.

It was the dark time just before dawn, but the moment she opened the box and took out the sapphire, the hearth was lit by a warm blue glow that emanated from the center of the stone itself.

This is me, she whispered, her magic speaking. *This is my center. I am the butterfly. It is time for me to transform myself into the greatest of all magicians.* Then, she admitted to herself, *I'm scared.*

It's my caution, not my fear, she reminded herself. *And it is from my caution that my power comes,* she affirmed, repeating Merlin's words.

She knew with a knowing and a certainty that went beyond all thought, all emotion, that today was hers alone.

And so she rose from the hearth, tucked the stone in her belt and went outside to assemble her people . . . .

But they were already assembled! The villagers had gathered and all the people of the land, armed with picks, shovels, scythes, and rakes, staffs and sticks, and whatever else they had been able to find, with their anger and fear combined. The animals were there too.

The king and queen were just arriving, with the guards and courtiers who were yet faithful to them. They were standing back to one side, safely out of the milieu. Their early morning attendants had seen from out the castle windows all those assembled here.

Alannah looked out across the plain in the direction of Iona's mountain. The hordes were gathered there, and before them stood the courtiers that sided with Utrek.

From even at this distance, she sensed their discomfort and fear. She knew they had wanted to win the battle for their share of the spoils, but now she could tell they were not so sure. They had never seen the hordes before, nor their daunting numbers.

Alannah felt as if someone had punched her in the belly. She was not expecting this, not so immediately. She had planned on gathering the people and explaining to them gently so their fears would not be so great.

"Fight them! Fight them!" the people shouted now, bringing her to the present. They were joined by the howling and screeching and bellowing of the animals. "Conquer them, for all time! Kill them!"

But inside Alannah heard, *Love them. Love them.*

But how? she wondered.

"Love them!" she cried, not realizing she had spoken out loud. A hush rippled across the masses. All speech stopped. All eyes stared. Even the king and queen, whom she secretly knew now to be her birth parents, looked at her askance.

She heard, *You must go into the world and create change.*

She asked silently, *How can I possibly do this?*

You will know when the time comes, she heard, and a ripple of fear ran up her spine at the idea of it.

I feel so alone.

Believe in your light and in your magic, even if you don't feel it, she remembered.

The hordes of the word-beings were marching now, closer and closer, thousands of them, and more coming behind. Their faces were cruel and distorted, laughing and jeering, their eyes ice cold and piercing, spittle flying from their misshapen mouths.

They stamped their feet as they came, calling out shaming names at the pathetic gathering before them. They wondered why their leader, the witch Iona, sent out so many—against one girl and a throng of villagers and courtiers and animals.

Alannah stood her ground before them, weaponless.

The villagers stood all around her, their only weapons the tools of their trades. She could hear them shifting uncomfortably from foot to foot, trying to hide their fear of what was to come, surely the slaughter of them all.

She had asked them to trust her. She spoke now. "Trust me," she said, more for herself than for anyone else, for she too was almost witless with fear. She held her head high, unconsciously humming nervously to herself, as she scanned the hordes, looking at them for the first time as individual beings.

It came to her that she recognized their jeering and their laughing in her very soul. Alannah realized that her fear was old and, at the same time, she knew so much more now than she had in those lives long ago, when she had first felt it.

Then she looked around her more closely. Queen Esmerelda hovered above her, and all of her realm. The faeries were not giggling now. Rather, they were fierce in their loyalty and their support of her. They hung in the air all around her in readiness, awaiting her command.

The trolls were there supporting her, smiling shyly as she acknowledged them. Dante circled above, slowly flapping his wings, drawing attention to himself, but staying on the periphery, knowing this was her day. The earth rumbled beneath her feet. *You are not alone,* she heard, and she knew that the dragon realm was awake and offering its invisible support.

And then she heard, *You can do this. I have complete faith in you.* It was Arete's voice and it was her own, white witch and sorceress herself now—and she knew that, no matter what happened, it would be *true*.

What she didn't know was what she was going to do to win this day. She only knew, with all of her heart and soul, that she was born for this day, this very moment, and it was time. She reached into her belt, felt for the sapphire, and took a deep breath. There was a warm touch on her heart, and she knew the Lady of the Earth was with her too. Alannah smiled faintly, strengthened by all the love and support around her.

Then she raised her face and arms to the sky, still humming under her breath, and waited for what was to come.

28 *Alannah's Song*

Even before Alannah could speak, she hummed. It was always the same tune absent-mindedly hummed under her breath, though she wasn't even aware that she did so.

It was the tune Dante sang without sound the night her dream self first met him, calling to her. It was the song the muses gave her at her creation. It was the song the Great Dragon had told her about. A song of pure joy.

Wherever she went, she hummed the same tune, hauntingly beautiful, the intricate strains of its melody floating on the winds and on the wings of butterflies and faeries, up through the valleys, across the fields, and into the mountains, subtly entrancing its magic into all who stood in its wake.

The notes spoke of the joy she was made of in her very soul. Her own very special magic was the magic of that joy. Wherever the tune was heard, it created a subtle enchantment, and the hearer picked it up and began to hum it too. In all those so enchanted, something changed for the better.

Over time, as Alannah grew, the tune began to spread across the kingdom without anyone remarking on the fact.

All who heard it simply wondered for a moment where it had come from, yet their hearts were lifted, smiles appeared on their faces, and light and joy shone in their eyes. It was always something sung under the breath or absently whistled while working on something else, but wherever it crept up, the singer as well as the environment were gently transformed.

The courtiers, when this happened, began to wonder what had taken over their servants, but only momentarily before they turned their thoughts back to more important things, like who had more jewels or splendor of gowns or favor with the council that ruled the king and queen.

It was no wonder then that, on the day of the Great Battle, when Alannah raised her arms and her face to the heavens, in her deep concentration on what was before her, she began to hum the tune under her breath.

Those of the kingdom close around her heard her humming. They prodded those next to them and began to hum the tune too. And so on throughout her small army, until all who had heard the tune all of Alannah's life and had learned it and grown it in their hearts, now joined their voices to hers.

The strains of the joy formed a growing force all its own, filled with hope and light and love, as strong and invincible as the castle walls themselves, a force to be reckoned with now, facing Iona's hordes.

The harmonies and nuances of the joined voices had never been so hauntingly beautiful, powerful, or ethereal. It was this fact that brought Alannah back to herself, for she knew at last what her purpose was.

Taking a deep breath, she filled her lungs with the joy she was spun from and, for the first time, she sang the tune out loud, her beautiful soprano voice imparting all the joy she had ever known. It rang out above all the others, clear, pure, strong, and *true*, across the mountains and valley and rivers, and across the great plain, as if it had sprouted wings of its own.

Her heart opened wide, filling the joy with all the ingredients of her making, adding goodness and light, laughter and love, right into the song. And it all came spilling—flooding—out of her heart, right into the sea of the hordes that stood before her.

As she sang, she began to look into the eyes of what all others were calling the enemy. And then, slowly, without her realizing it, her arms rose even higher, as if gathering the earth itself, and the love she felt there. Her palms faced out to the multitudes, and it was as if time stood still once again.

Without knowing why, their weapons still raised, those who had been called the enemy did not attack but waited instead, mesmerized, for inside a shifting was taking place.

Alannah looked into the eyes of each of them, into their very souls. Tears began to fall down her cheeks, as she saw that these were the ones who had offered themselves as souls, long ago, to be the great legion of the shadow, part of that shining beauty that was the Source of all things.

Her joy surged up—and with it, goodness and light, laughter and love—from out of the earth through her body, out of the heavens through her heart, and slowly, gently, she breathed it through song in all directions. She sent it through her eyes, as she looked at each one in the legions before her, and she poured it from her fingertips.

It was a whoosh of magic so powerful that across the land was heard a sound like a great ice storm, as slowly and gently, one by one, the frozen hearts thawed, tears fell, weapons dropped, and that great legion that was called "the enemy" began to come back to the light that it once was.

With magic coursing through her every cell now, pulsing, pouring, so that all she was, was magic, Alannah whispered to this legion, just as the words came to her, *Allow love in, Allow joy in*, like an ancient invocation.

She remembered now—as if waking from a long time ago—the meaning of the sacred text in the ancient language inlaid in silver on the butterfly box the trolls had given her. *You are joy. You are love. You are one with the Source of all things.*

And she saw in that moment, each member of the horde remembering with her.

They fell to their knees with the grief of all they had done, and yet somehow they knew that it had been for the good of all. For did they not show themselves to be that which all were, in part—the shadow part of all of us? And did they not have courage in that first offering, so long ago?

As more and more remembered, more of the hordes came forward and remembered with them. It was as if the entire legion of the shadow, from all parts of the world, out of the wind and stars and trees and caves and tunnels, all came for this remembering. All fell to their knees, in their mingled grief and joy, as well as in their gratitude to this one girl, who seemed to them at first so small and powerless, moments ago.

Some of their number merely dissolved back into the ethers where they had come from, before they were formed from Iona's words, wretched souls freed now.

The villagers too were moved to tears, for they did not expect this. Even though they loved Alannah, there had been that in her that had separated her from them, which they did not understand in their simplicity.

Slowly, as if coming out of a trance, Alannah lowered her arms. She blinked and looked around her, at both sides that had become one. She smiled weakly. Her eyes had a faraway look, as she remembered the lifetimes of those souls.

Slowly, one by one, as they dropped their weapons, tears streaming down their misshapen faces, those of the hordes bowed their heads in a gesture swearing allegiance to this beautiful and marvelous being who at last had touched them and melted the hearts they did not even know they had.

And in the moment of their swearing this new allegiance to goodness and light and joy, they were released from the old vows and, miraculously, their features transformed into beauty and wholeness. They lost their misshapenness and became new, dressed in the simple light-colored garments of long ago.

As she beheld this happening, Alannah was so deeply moved that tears of gratitude and love streamed down her cheeks. In the midst of all this, she felt someone gently slipping his hand around hers. She turned her head to find Tarek at her side. He was here.

She closed her eyes for a moment and sighed quietly, not having imagined that her joy could be greater. "Tarek," she whispered and stroked his face. "I missed you." Even now, he could feel traces of the magic in her hands, and he marveled at this woman whom he loved so much.

Then they were in each other's arms, and suddenly the song changed to a cheer from both sides, of gladness for their reunion. They raised their hands to the sky, joined for all to see. In the midst of the clamor of the cheer, as if they were in a private bubble that enclosed just the two of them, Alannah whispered to Tarek, loud enough for him to hear her over the cheering, "What happened? What made you come today?"

"I realized that my path is my own, and only I can take it, wherever it leads me," Tarek whispered back. "There's no blame here. Forgive me."

"There's nothing to forgive," grinned Alannah, touching his arm fondly. She looked to the people then and to the hordes and added, "I'm so glad you're here. Can we talk later?"

He nodded his head and said, "I missed you too." They smiled at each other and then joined the people again.

Slowly and hesitantly, the individual members of the hordes came forward, and the villagers, freshly filled with the joy of the tune, reached out their hands to them, murmuring, "A welcome to you," or "Greetings to you, neighbor," or "All joy to you."

On another plane, in that place called *Far Away*, those who were there watched as waves of love rippled across the land and spread all around the planet and into the universes, and a collective sigh was heard.

"All is well now," said Merlin.

"At last," agreed Arete and Dante in unison, all three able to straddle all planes in one moment.

"And finally, the old belief that magic doesn't exist is releasing from the planet," exclaimed Merlin, gratified.

"Yes!" they all exclaimed together. "So it was written."

And so it was. And that change, invoked and first created in that ancient circle of *Far Away* and *Long Ago* was at last coming *true*.

It is time now for love, joy, and magic to spread across the planet and embed into the hearts of all beings in all universes. And so these words rang across the ethers, doing just that into eternity.

29 *The Great Feast*

A feast was quickly planned for the evening, to take place outside on the castle grounds so that all could take part, including Dante. And in the hubbub and flurry of the "Great Feast," as it was later called down the generations, Tarek pulled Alannah aside and whisked her into that very same herb garden where they had learned the truth of who they were.

There, he stopped and nervously let go of her hand.

Alannah gazed at him longingly, her heart thumping to have him so close, not knowing what he would say, but hoping he felt the same as she did.

And then he burst out, "I was never so proud of you, Alannah. I'm sorry I was such a fool and that it took me so long to speak to you. I don't care what my role is in the kingdom. I'm not whole without you. You're my light, and I don't want to live without you. You mean everything to me." He swallowed, hesitated, then added, "I love you."

His eyes searched hers, as he paused. "I know I'm below you in stature now," he added, "but will you marry me?"

Alannah could barely see through her tears, she was so filled with joy. She pressed a finger to his lips and whispered, "Be quiet. You're not a fool. And I love you too. And yes," she added, reaching up and kissing him gently on the lips. "I will marry you." And then she grinned, "I've wanted to for a long time." With that, he swept her into his arms and deepened the kiss, holding her tight, as though he'd never let her go, and the joy and the love they shared knew no bounds.

Suddenly, the air above them was filled with the song without sound, and they looked up. There, circling above them was Dante flying close, with Merlin and Arete on his back. All three were smiling, if you can imagine a dragon's smile! And then they heard a raucous cawing. It was Spoke, Arete's crow, perched on the garden wall, laughing down at them.

The trolls joined them in the herb garden then and Queen Esmerelda and the faeries too. Word spread, and the villagers came next, and then the king and the queen, looking somewhat baffled.

There were so many beings in the herb garden enclosure that the king suggested they all move out to the royal grounds again where the merriment was being held. And so they did.

Dante circled down and found a clearing big enough to land, and Merlin and Arete alit. Spoke landed on Arete's shoulder almost before she reached the ground, and she pushed him off, pretending to grumble at him as usual. Then she stepped away and disappeared into the throng.

Soon after, there was a disturbance in the crowd, as it parted to make way for Arete coming back with a plump old woman, with white hair and a kind face. They came to stand before the king and queen and curtsied to them both.

"But who is this?" asked the queen. "I feel I know you from somewhere. Who are you?" she asked the old woman kindly.

"I am Deidre, the princess's midwife, if it please my lady," the old woman responded humbly, curtsying again.

"What do you mean 'the princess's midwife?'" asked the queen, shocked. "We had a son, not a daughter!"

"I beg your pardon, my lady, but if you will look behind the left ear of this girl here, who saved the kingdom," she said, pointing at Alannah, "you will see a tiny butterfly mark there. I saw it at her birth, and then I was banished from the castle till now. I don't know why I was banished, or why I am here now either. But that's the truth, my lady. I stake my life on it."

"What is the meaning of this?" asked the king now too, his face red with fury. "Take her away!" he ordered the guards standing nearby.

Both Alannah and Arete cried, "Wait!" They looked at each other. Alannah reached into her belt and pulled out the butterfly sapphire, whispering to Arete, "Is this the right time?" knowing it was, even as she asked it.

Arete gave her an answering nod, but before she could speak, Tarek stepped forward instead. "It is true, my king and my queen," he said.

They looked at him as if he had lost his mind. He had always called them "Mother" and "Father."

"What—" sputtered the king.

"Let me explain," interrupted Tarek. "Please."

And so he told them of the switch at birth, and then Merlin came forward, and Dante sidled as close as he could. Arete joined them, and they explained the rest. Between all of them, they proved Alannah's identity as the true princess by showing them the butterfly mark.

All that time, Alannah was holding the sapphire and it was glowing hotter and hotter in her hand. She kept having to switch hands until, finally, she couldn't stand it any longer, so she held it up to the king and queen, to show them.

There was a great clap of thunder, and the sapphire splintered open in Alannah's hand and, just for a moment, it became a bright glittering silvery wand made of thousands of tiny individual sparkles of magic hovering in the air.

And then it transformed itself into a myriad of blue butterflies that flitted from ear to ear to all the people of the kingdom, reminding them of what was *true*.

Suddenly, the people remembered the particulars of the birth as Tarek and Alannah really were—a princess born to the king and queen, and a son born to the woodcutter and his wife.

"You will always be my parents in my eyes, if you will have me," ended Tarek, "but I am not a prince."

"You will always be my son, Tarek," said the queen. "And mine too, my son," added the king. Turning to the queen, he said, his eyes sparkling with amusement, "but are we not fortunate, my dear, and delighted to learn that we also now have a daughter?"

He turned to Alannah and said, "Come, daughter, let us welcome you with open arms," gesturing to her to join them.

There were smiles and embraces all around, and then the crowd parted again. There stood Jacob and Anna, their faces stained with tears, thinking they had lost both children to the castle.

Knowing who the couple was, the king looked at the queen and a silent message passed between them. She nodded her head, beaming at them. "You must live here at the castle," she said, "and see your daughter and your son every day, for they are both to us all, are they not?

"What position would you like to hold for the kingdom, now that you will live here?" she asked.

But Jacob looked to Anna, holding his hat in his hands nervously, and they both looked to Alannah. She smiled gently at them and kissed them each on the cheek. "Mama. Papa. Nothing will ever change my love for you. You taught me so much, and I have loved you for so long. Let us remain as we are, even if I am the princess now."

She turned to the king and queen and asked, "I think I am right in guessing that Jacob and Anna would like to stay in their hut, is that right, Papa?" Jacob nodded at Alannah, tears of pride and love in his eyes, as he beheld this girl he raised from a babe. "And I think also," added Alannah, "that he would like to stay as a woodcutter."

Again, Jacob nodded his head, and he and Anna shared a look of such warmth and happiness that it was obvious they both wanted the same thing.

"It shall be as you wish," affirmed the king, "but if you should ever want for anything, you must let me know. Will you?" he asked Jacob, his eyes sparkling mischievously, daring the man to answer for himself.

Jacob was completely unruffled by the king's demeanor and replied in his quiet way, "Yes, Your Highness, I will."

But then he looked over at the trolls, thought for a moment, and added, "There may be one thing though."

"What is that?" asked the king, surprised.

"There are many poor in the kingdom, and the stores are almost gone. I wonder if you would ask the trolls not to require tolls at the bridges?"

The trolls stared at each other in alarm, but then they looked into Alannah's smiling face, and Selwik looked at his grandson Dorin, both grumbling-mumbling-smiling, and they made a quick decision. Selwik agreed, "Yes. We will stop all of our tolling. And, not only that, we will put our fortune in trust to Alannah to dole out as she wishes, or to Tarek, if that is the right thing to do. We trust them both."

Alannah went to the king and queen and whispered something to them, and they whispered back. Then she stepped back and smiled at the trolls again.

"I can already see," said the king, grinning, "that this maiden has much wisdom. She has asked that you, Selwik, be made the treasurer of the land, and Dorin will be your apprentice. Would you agree to that?"

The old troll was dumbfounded, looking to his grandson and the others. They mumbled and grumbled amongst themselves quietly. Then, after a nod of their heads, he came forward and said, "I will be honored, Your Highness. Thank you.

"And perhaps, the first thing we could do is use some of our funds to buy stores from neighboring kingdoms to replenish those we have lost? Would that meet with your approval, Your Highnesses?"

The king and queen readily agreed, doubly pleased now with their new daughter and her wise suggestion. Selwik thanked them, smiled at Alannah, and stepped back to join the other trolls.

Again, the crowd parted. With halting steps, an old gnarled woman came forward, dressed all in black, her head hanging with shame. Alannah immediately went to her and hugged her. "Iona," she said. "You came."

Dante sidled up, and Arete and Merlin too stepped forward, but they were hesitant, as she was. "Will you forgive me?" she asked the king and queen. "Will you forgive me?"

she asked Dante and Arete and Merlin. "I didn't know what I was doing, not until this girl here came to visit me."

King Heinrich and Queen Isobel looked over her head to Dante and Merlin and Arete, and then to Alannah. They had seen Iona leading the hordes, but they watched, curious to see what progressed.

"What have you learned?" they heard Arete gently ask Iona, before they could make a decree.

"I don't ever want to lose my center again," answered Iona. "I lost myself. I can't ever do that again. I miss my healing powers, but even more, I miss myself and you. I miss loving and being loved." She sighed. "It wasn't until Alannah came to my cave that I remembered what it felt like. Will you forgive me?" she asked again, all around. "I never meant to hurt anyone, not at first."

As if in answer, the crowd parted one last time. Haltingly on little stick legs, snuffling the grass here and there, came a little fawn, its front paws stained black with ink. Iona cried, "Fawn! It's you! You're you again!" She ran to hug him.

Then she looked to Alannah, and Arete and Merlin and Dante, and last to the king and queen, and she saw the gentle understanding in all of their faces. She saw their love. The tears began to run down her face, as she said, "I was so alone. Thank you, Alannah."

Just then, Alannah felt a strange vibration, like a shock wave, touching her hand. Looking down, she saw grasped in her palm, a beautiful, silvery-blue, sparkling wand, vibrating and bristling with magic. She gasped with delight and looked up at Arete.

"You deserve it, my dear girl," said Arete, reaching out to Alannah and stroking her hair. "You proved yourself today. You proved that, even in your fear, your love and joy shone through. You held to your center. Congratulations!"

"Thank you," replied Alannah, shyly, but then she cried, "Isn't it beautiful? And I know just what I want to do with it!" With that, she wielded it high above her head.

Only those of magic could see a flood of ancient letters swirling in the air. And only those of magic knew the words they spelled, before they turned into what all could see: a flock of blue butterflies that swooped and fluttered then landed gently all over Iona, so she was standing in a pale blue cloud. Allow love in. Allow joy in.

Before everyone's eyes, Iona's body straightened, her hair darkened to black, still with some grey, her skin lost its wrinkles, and she became who she truly was, a handsome woman of middle age—forthright, strong, and noble of bearing.

"Don't forget yourself again, sister," roared Dante quietly.

"Don't forget we are here for you, sister," declared Merlin, a twinkle in his eyes. "We are just so glad to have you back!"

Arete walked up to her and hugged her, saying nothing, tears running down her cheeks too. Finally, she whispered, "I have missed you, sister. For so long. Welcome home."

After the blue butterflies had finished their transformation of Iona, they merged into the wand again, and it took its rightful place then in Alannah's hand. She grinned to see it, knowing though that she must never let it be a crutch, but rather a reminder of all that had come to pass.

Her eyes sought out Arete's then, and Arete grinned broadly at her, saying, "I am so proud of you, Alannah, or should I say 'white witch—sorceress,' for that is who you are now, my dear!" And then she hugged Alannah with all the strength of her magic and her love and joy too.

From that day on, Alannah's wand, when she wasn't using it, was displayed in the great hall of the castle so all could see, reminding the people of this fateful day. Later, the king and queen commissioned a painting of her holding her wand.

Towards the end of the Great Feast, Iona found a time when all was merriment, and no one would notice her. She searched out Utrek, and beckoned to him to follow her to the royal dais for an audience with the king and queen.

"It was my fault partly," she admitted to the royal couple, "that Utrek plotted so to gain power and control over the kingdom. I added to his greed with my magic and used him to further my own ends. I have released him, and I am in the hopes that we can both learn from our mistakes. Please, do not judge him as harshly as you might. I was wrong."

With that, the king nodded, "I will forgive you both, if you both promise to learn from your mistakes and help me run the kingdom, rather than running it into the ground. I will have you swear your allegiance to me, here and now."

Utrek was deeply moved that, after all he had done, he was being forgiven, and he knelt before the king, Iona at his side. They swore on their hearts, and on the Source of all things, to uphold the law and stay *true* to the king and the kingdom.

Somehow, magic-wise, Alannah had heard this interchange, and she was glad. Just as she was turning back to find Tarek in the crowds, she felt a light touch on her shoulder. It was the faery queen, her wings rapidly flitting, balancing there.

"Hello, Queen Esmerelda!" cried Alannah, both surprised and delighted. "What can I do for you?"

In her silvery voice, the queen whispered, "I just want to remind you that words still have power. They can still hurt. That will not change. Remember this, my dear," and with that, she flitted away, sketching the shape of a heart in the air with her faery dust, her laughter tinkling as she went.

Alannah knew she would never forget, for humans still had much to learn, but she had faith in humanity. She wove her way through the crowd then to join her handsome prince, and to tell him of the faery queen's message.

Iona, Arete, Dante, and Merlin were all reunited, and Iona was no longer alone.

It gladdened Alannah's heart to see all those she loved reconciled and happy.

So it was that the truth became known about Alannah and Tarek, and the story of their births spread
far across the land to neighboring kingdoms and
beyond. The people were glad for the young couple and felt
safe for the first time in generations, for they loved Tarek,
no matter what his new stature was. They loved Alannah
too, and they trusted them both to rule wisely and fairly
when the time came.

Their wedding was planned in a way to make sure that
the people from far and wide could attend, for their story had
inspired much curiosity. At the same time, the newly pur-
chased stores could be delivered.

Of all those of royalty who came from afar, there was one
who did not smile, nor did she seem to truly attend. She was
the Queen Willow, a beautiful woman of mature years, with
a gossamer gown that floated around her, her hair graced
with flowers, rather than a crown.

In the midst of the festivities, Alannah was struck by the
queen's sadness and went to her and asked her gently what
was wrong. All Queen Willow said was, "I worry for my son.

He keeps to himself and hides away. I wonder what will become of him and what will become of our kingdom when it comes time for him to reign."

Alannah laid her hand on her arm and said, "I am so sorry. Is there anything I can do?"

The queen answered, "I don't know. I just don't know. Your kingdom is so far from ours, but I thank you for your kindness and your compassion. I am sure that in time, all will be well." And with that, she seemed to muster herself, bowed her head, and walked away.

Alannah knew the time was not right to assist her, and yet she had a strong feeling their paths would cross again. There was so much else to do in her own land, and this was her wedding day, after all.

So she went to join Tarek, her own beloved, her heart quickening with joy. They shared their happiness with all those they loved, knowing that the vows they made that day activated hope and a new beginning for this land and these people who had suffered so.

After the wedding, Dante circled high above the castle, his song reaching far across the mountains and plains. He landed on the grounds, bent his great neck to look right into the eyes of his darling Alannah, and said, "Are you ready, Princess? Tarek?"

Alannah smiled and patted his neck, as she had so long ago when they first met, and she climbed on, beckoning Tarek to follow. And so he did, wrapping his arms around her and softly kissing her neck. She loved the warmth of him there and felt whole and safe, knowing she was loved.

Once they were both settled, Dante spread his great blue-black wings and began to rise into the sky. Up they went, sailing higher and higher, the people below them craning their necks to watch, and cheering and laughing for them in delight.

It was with fresh eyes that Alannah and Tarek looked below to the farms and forests, lakes and oceans, all at peace at last. They felt hopeful now that they could make it better, and they were glad in their hearts.

When they returned finally from their days of exploration and their nights of joy, the former prince Tarek and the new princess were appointed the head advisors to the king and queen.

Soon after, seeing the natural wisdom that resided in the hearts of the newly married couple, King Heinrich and Queen Isobel decided to hand over their thrones to the young couple, as the *true* rulers of the land. As such, one of the first things the new king and queen did was to make sure that the people were educated about the effects of the words they used.

The courtiers and advisors who had vied for themselves were banished, demoted, or given another chance, depending on their amenability to being under a rule that was *true* in all ways. Rannulf built and headed an army that protected, rather than attacked, and he became King Tarek's right hand man. Utrek, knowing all that he did about the workings of the kingdom, used his knowledge for good now and assisted both King Tarek and Rannulf in promoting safety and peace in the land.

All of this happened over a year ago. It was spring now, and Queen Alannah sat on the grass in the very same courtyard garden where she had first learned she was a princess.

Tulip and daffodil shoots were peeking out of the earth. The air was filled with the sweet fragrances of hyacinths, lilies of the valley, and crocuses. All around her was alive with birds flitting back and forth, busy nesting and feeding their young.

She smiled to herself to think how blessed she was, and she lost herself in thought for a moment until a tiny bell-like gurgle drew her attention to a different kind of sweetness lying beside her. It was her delightful daughter Sophia, born mere months ago, her tiny fingers and toes waving in the air as the infant princess tried to catch the faeries who teased and flitted around her, laughing.

She has magic too, thought Alannah, glad to be alive to see this perfect child whom she loved more than life itself, with her petal-pink lips, blue-gray eyes, rosy cheeks, and hair the color of winter beech leaves.

"Oh, you!" cried the young queen, as she reached down to tickle and tease her daughter. The faeries flew up for a moment as she did so and then settled back down to land again on the tiny girl's nose and ears, fingers and toes.

Epilogue

The babe let out a squeal of infant laughter, and the queen sighed to hear it. "The kingdom is at peace now. All is well," she whispered. She raised her face to the sun and the birds and the faeries and the sweet scent of flowers, knowing at the same time that humans would be humans, and accepting that.

"But for now!" she said and scooped the squealing babe up from the sprinkling of faery dust that fell all around her, holding her close, and told her she loved her.

The young King Tarek looked on from the arched stone entrance to the herb garden and smiled to himself to see his wife and child at such peace. He too felt blessed, in all things, but mostly in these two most important beings in his life. Just looking at them made him feel whole.

"I wonder how Queen Willow is," he heard his wife murmur to the child, looking into her eyes and smiling. "Shall we go visit her some time soon, dearest?" she asked Sophia, tickling the baby, who giggled and cooed in response.

"Maybe we can find out why her son keeps to himself. And maybe we can help her. I would so love that, my dearest." And then, she laughed and held the child close, nuzzling her, nose to nose, saying, "All is well, sweet one."

Tarek heard this, and he was glad for the land and his people, for it was still Alannah who had so much magic, and he trusted her. With that, he went quietly back inside to the ruling of the kingdom, his heart filled with love.

And so the kingdom was reigned in peace for many generations, and everyone lived happily ever after. And the tale ends, my dears, for now anyway.

The old one looks to the child asleep in her lap and to the other children asleep on the sweet-smelling, herb-strewn floor. Her eyes crinkle with the telling, knowing that what she has told is *true.*

One child, a little girl of perhaps three or four, with green eyes the color of magic, looks up into her face, and they share a secret, unspoken for now, but for the magic that weaves it into their two souls. The old one winks, and the little girl smiles to herself, and she too falls asleep.

But the old one is wide-awake now, for there are faeries tugging at her hair and whispering in her ear, wanting her to tell another tale, wanting more.

"Not yet," she whispers, rocking in her chair. "Not yet, but soon."

And then, she too is asleep, breathing in the sweetness of the child in her lap and the love in her heart for them all.

The End

When I was growing up, history was never my favorite subject. I could never take in the dates and names and facts I was supposed to learn, because they had no meaning for me. I lived in a world of faery tales and dreams, and still do partly, even as an adult.

I always believed that, if history had been taught with stories and movies and books, like Johnny Tremain, I would have understood and remembered.

So, here I tell a story in the hopes that it may both enlighten and empower my readers, and that you will remember how it feels to BE Alannah! To feel the power of knowing the rightness inside that is your own *true.*

May joy fill your days, and a song fill your heart, a song of who you are.

About the Author

eslie Brooks has a BA in Art, a minor in Poetry, an MA in Counseling Psychology, and is a Master RoHun Therapist and soul worker.

Her first three published books are of a spiritual, inspirational nature, following the process of her learning and enlightenment, by way of teaching tools that might assist others in their own evolution.

This is her first magical fantasy in print. She has written two others, *The Christmas Santa Fell Asleep* (originally written at the age of eighteen), and *The Magic Willow* (originally written in 1990), both of which she is in the process of reworking for publication in the near future.

Another fantasy that is already weaving itself into physicality is *The Salt Princess,* which is an adaptation of an old faerytale. Leslie can't wait for the story to emerge so she can find out what the *true* ending is, at last!

She believes that life is about magic and doing what you love to do best!

For more, see Leslie's amazon author page at Leslie Brooks/amazon author page.

A b o u t   t h e   C o v e r

When it was time to look for the cover, I spent hours and days and weeks, looking through images online. Finally, after all that searching, I found the artwork of Ruth Sanderson at www.ruthsanderson.com.

Her image was perfect. It shows the golden being that Alannah is, her magic, and her goodness and brightness.

I was astounded when I learned that Ruth's studio is in Easthampton, Massachusetts, not far from where I live.

I cannot thank Ruth enough for this wonderful image!

And of course, it's the painting that hangs in the great hall of the castle on that other magical plane where Tarek and Alannah live happily ever after!

—Leslie Brooks

AN EXCERPT FROM *THE MAGIC WILLOW*,

coming in 2017...

Chapter 1

A young girl named Aife sat alone reading on a bench by the willow tree in the meadow behind her family's cottage. Her book fell to her lap as she daydreamed. Sometimes, when she looked into the old trunk, she thought she saw her grandmother's face smiling down at her, so patient and kind. Or maybe it was an old queen, or a magic sorceress who could concoct a solution that would make her speak like everyone else.

Today, the pale green branches seemed to whisper, "Come to me and let me hold you and soothe your worries. You are too young to be so sad." The leaves of a long branch brushed her shoulder, and she turned to look up. In the old gnarled trunk, she saw her grandmother's face clearly now, but this time it seemed actually to smile.

She got up from the bench and rubbed her eyes to make sure she wasn't dreaming. She walked slowly towards the willow until she was face to face with its worn old trunk. She was confused and felt silly and yet drawn to the rough leather-like maze of its hundred-year surface. She felt so tired and dejected. She couldn't stand another minute of her lonely life. And then she started to cry, leaning against the tree. A soft gentle voice began to hum a beautiful angel tune, like the lullaby of a young mother in awe of her first child. The sweeping branches wrapped around her and soothed her, as her grandmother used to do before she died.

Aife raised her face, wet with tears, to see if the face was still there, and to her amazement, a door appeared in the trunk and swung open inviting her inside.

She hesitated for a moment. *How is this possible?* she asked herself. *I must be dreaming.* But then she thought, *If I'm dreaming, there's no harm in going in. And, if I'm not . . .* She couldn't think of an answer, nor did she want to.

She stepped through the door and found herself inside a white marble palace as high as the biggest cathedral. Its walls were covered with huge, beautifully rich paintings in red and purple and blue and yellow, of princes and princesses riding white horses, of gold and pearls and rubies and emeralds. In the middle of the white marble floor was a rectangular pool inlaid with blue stones and coral, full of fish of every pattern and color imaginable.

The water boiled and frothed, and a big fish-fin slapped down and splashed her. Then a mermaid appeared. Her face was the color of a new white rose with the slightest blush of pink, and her hair was blue-black like magic. Her scales were peacock-blue-green and glittered like silver coins in moonlight.

"Welcome to our world," the mermaid said. "My name is Elsa. What's yours?"

Elsa's voice was like a wave rushing in over tiny pebbles, like a flock of sandpipers running before the tide. Everything about her was beautiful, but Aife especially liked Elsa's voice because it seemed so fluid, so smooth. How could she possibly answer, and how could she keep her secret?

35105030R00144

Made in the USA
Middletown, DE
19 September 2016